"I've been awa[...] time," he said. [...] you think I am.

"I may not be the woman you think I am," she countered. "If you think about me at all," she added sheepishly.

"Hard to forget someone you meet on top of a bridge."

He saw a shiver go through her as she turned to stare out the windshield. She looked very enticing with her hair all mussed and her lips slightly parted. Another time, another place and Jack might have responded to the subtle invitation in her smile. But a hookup was the last thing he needed. He'd come to town to poke a hornet's nest. Depending on what he found, things could get ugly. Sides might have to be chosen. After all was said and done, he'd return to Houston while Olive would still have to live here.

Jack knew only too well what it was like to be a pariah in Pine Lake.

away from here for a long
time, he told her. "I may not be the man
that Michael was."

PINE LAKE

AMANDA STEVENS

Recycling programs
for this product may
not exist in your area.

ISBN-13: 978-1-335-72126-6

Pine Lake

Printed in U.S.A.

Amanda Stevens is an award-winning author of over fifty novels, including the modern gothic series, The Graveyard Queen. Her books have been described as eerie and atmospheric, "a new take on the classic ghost story." Born and raised in the rural South, she now resides in Houston, Texas, where she enjoys binge-watching, bike riding and the occasional margarita.

Books by Amanda Stevens

Harlequin Intrigue

Pine Lake

MIRA Books

The Graveyard Queen

The Restorer
The Kingdom
The Prophet
The Visitor
The Sinner
The Awakening

Visit the Author Profile page at Harlequin.com.

CAST OF CHARACTERS

Jack King—Suspected of killing his high school girlfriend, Jack left town fifteen years ago, vowing never to return. But a phone call from an old friend lures him back to Pine Lake and to the secrets lurking beneath the murky surface.

Olive Belmont—A sleepwalker since adolescence, Olive finds herself pulled back time and again to the old Pine Lake bridge. For fifteen years, memories of a murder have remained trapped within her subconscious. Now another young woman is dead and a killer is closing in.

Anna Grayson—She was the most beautiful girl in Pine Lake dating the most popular boy in high school. She seemed to have it all until her penchant for secrets put her in the crosshairs of a killer.

Nathan Bolt—He was one of Jack King's best friends, but like all the others in town, he turned his back when Jack needed him the most. Now he needs Jack's help and he's willing to give up another friend—and an old secret—to insure Jack's return to Pine Lake.

Tommy Driscoll—He and Nathan and Jack were best buddies until Anna's murder shattered their friendship. He's now the sheriff of Caddo County, but his badge does little to conceal his vices.

Beth Driscoll—She has no delusions about her husband's fidelity, but the secrets of the past bind them together.

Mona Sutton—The high school guidance counselor has been hiding a deep, dark secret of her own.

Jamie Butaud—A seemingly innocent tattoo connects her murder to Anna Grayson's.

Marc Waller—Jamie's hotheaded boyfriend has been up to no good.

Chapter One

It was an ordinary day. Which made the phone call all the more extraordinary.

Jack King wasn't in the best of moods to begin with. He'd been stuck inside since early morning and boredom had worn down his patience. Even on the rare instances when he found himself in between assignments, he could usually rustle up something that would keep him out of the office. No chore was too tedious so long as it put distance between him and his cluttered desk.

For the past five years, he'd been working for the Blackthorn Agency, a high-profile consultant and security organization headquartered in Houston, Texas. Jack worked in Black Watch, the division tasked with state and municipal government oversight, including police departments. His particular expertise was in exposing corruption in cities large and small where the rot started at the head and worked its way down through the ranks. It wasn't a job for the faint of heart. Cops were notoriously territorial and they knew how to circle the wagons. But Jack enjoyed the challenge and he'd learned a long time ago how to watch his back.

That morning, he'd arrived at headquarters with the expectation of a new briefing. Instead, a mountain of delinquent paperwork and a stern warning from the man upstairs had kept him chained to his desk as his gaze strayed every few minutes to the clock on the wall outside his office. The day had seemed interminable.

Finally at six, he filed his last report, stood, stretched and walked out of his office, wishing the division manager a nice weekend. He was just getting off the elevator when his phone rang. He started to ignore it. Wished a thousand times later that he had. He didn't want to be called back upstairs because he'd dotted the wrong *i* or forgotten to cross a *t*. Whatever technicality needed his attention could damn well wait until Monday.

Still…

He slid the phone out of his pocket and checked the screen. No name, just a number. The area code and prefix pinged his alarm and he told himself again to ignore the call. He couldn't, of course. Curiosity niggled. He'd had no contact with anyone in his hometown in over fifteen years. He'd left Pine Lake the day after his high school graduation and his folks had fled a month later. Only his uncle Leon had remained to tough things out, but he'd passed away last spring. Jack hadn't even gone back for the funeral.

No good could come of that phone call. He knew that. But he pressed the phone to his ear anyway as he strode across the lobby, nodding to the security guard behind the desk on his way out.

"Hello," he said as he pushed open the glass door and stepped through into the early August heat.

"Jack? Jack King, right?"

Unease feathered along his spine. "Yes, this is Jack."

"You don't know who this is, do you? Little wonder. It's been a long time. Fifteen years to be exact." The caller fell silent. "Damn, this is a lot harder than I thought it would be. It's Nathan, Jack. Nathan Bolt."

Nathan Bolt. Now there was a name from his past. He and Jack and Tommy Driscoll had been best friends all through school. Blood brothers since kindergarten. Thick as thieves, Uncle Leon used to say. Until Nathan and Tommy had turned on Jack during their senior year. They'd given each other alibis for the night of Anna Grayson's murder, leaving Jack alone in the crosshairs of a ruthless sheriff.

With little evidence and zero suspects, the authorities had gone hard after Jack. He was the boyfriend, after all, and unlike Tommy and Nathan, he hadn't been able to produce an alibi. The harassment had continued for months, making him an outcast in the place where he'd lived his whole life. Even after an arrest had finally been made and an ex-con sent back to prison, the community had continued to shun him. In the ensuing years, Jack had done his best to forget about Pine Lake and everyone who lived there, but not a day went by that he didn't think about Anna. Not a day went by that he didn't wish for her the long and happy life she had deserved.

An image flashed through his head. Dark hair, dark eyes. A smile that could light up a stadium.

Sweat beaded on his brow. He wiped it away with the back of his hand.

"Hello? Jack? You there? Did I lose you?"

"I'm here," he said, though his instinct still was to end the call without giving Nathan a chance to explain why he had decided to make contact after so many years of silence. Or how he had gotten Jack's number in the first place. That probably wasn't too hard to figure out. He'd been Uncle Leon's attorney.

"You must be wondering why I'm calling," Nathan said.

"Did Leon give you my number?"

"Yes. We discussed certain things before he died. He said I should give you a call."

"What things?"

Another pause. "Did you get the letter I sent you about his estate?"

"I got it."

"I wondered. I never heard back from you. Things have been left hanging, but that's my fault. I should have followed up. And I should have called when it first happened. I'm sorry I didn't. I'm sorry about a lot of things." He sighed. "I don't imagine that cuts much ice with you."

"If this is about Leon's estate, you should talk to my dad," Jack said brusquely. "He'll give you whatever you need."

"If you read my letter, you know Leon left everything to you. The cabin, the little bit of cash he had in the bank. But this isn't about your uncle."

"Then what's it about?"

"I need to talk to you about Tommy."

It had started to rain, a light drizzle that spiked the humidity and turned the oily streets to glass. As if traffic wasn't bad enough on a Friday afternoon in downtown Houston. Jack pressed against the building to keep dry.

"Why would you need to talk to me about Tommy?"

"He's the Caddo County sheriff. Going on three years now. Leon must have told you about the last election. The accusations of fraud and intimidation. The way that vote went down left a lot of bad blood in this town."

"Leon and I didn't talk politics." They hadn't talked much at all in the past few years and that was on Jack. He'd let himself get too caught up in work because it was easier to focus on the greed and corruption of others than to dwell on his own shortcomings, including a failed marriage. If a day didn't go by without a thought of Anna, his ex-wife hardly ever crossed his mind. That undoubtedly said more about Jack than it did about her. Not her fault he had trust issues. Not for lack of trying that she couldn't breach his walls.

"I've done my research," Nathan was saying. "I know what you do at the Blackthorn Agency. You investigate police departments, right? You expose government corruption."

"Among other things."

"Leon said you were the best at what you do."

"Leon was biased."

"Maybe, but you always were the best at everything you set your mind to."

Was that an edge of the old jealousy rearing its ugly head? Jack and Tommy Driscoll had had a good-natured rivalry on the football field, but the competition with Nathan in the classroom hadn't been so amiable. Nathan needed to be the best and the brightest in order to prove his worth to his father. Jack needed the grades for a scholarship. His early acceptance to a top-tier school had been a bitter pill for Nathan to swallow, but that offer and most of the others had been rescinded when Anna's murder and the subsequent investigation had made the national news. And that had been a bitter pill for Jack to swallow.

"I know I'm catching you off guard," Nathan said. "But I didn't know who else to call. We've got a real problem up here, Jack. Drugs have taken over the whole damn county. Crack, meth, kush. And nobody has a mind to do anything about it. You can't imagine how bad it's gotten."

"I've worked on the border," Jack said. "I don't have to imagine how bad things can get."

"Well, sure. El Paso's one thing, but we're talking about Pine Lake. Last year alone, we had ten murders in Caddo County. *Ten.* Not a lot by big city standards, but you must remember how quiet this place once was."

He remembered, all right.

"Something's going on in our little town. Something bad. Used to be just a few random incidents, but now there's organization. Muscle. And I think Tommy's involved. In it up to his neck, is my guess."

"In what?"

"That's what I need you to find out."

"If you're looking to hire my firm, you'll have to go through the proper channels. I don't solicit work. I go where I'm told."

"I was hoping we could do this off the books. I'll pay you myself. Whatever you want."

"Not interested."

"Even if it could lead you to Anna's murderer?"

Nathan's words were like scissor points gouging a tender wound. "Her killer was sent to prison fifteen years ago."

"What if they pinned it on the wrong man? Have you ever considered that?"

More times than Jack cared to remember. He'd even made a trip to the Texas State Penitentiary a few years back to interview Wayne Foukes for himself. He'd come away more convinced than ever that

Foukes belonged behind bars. He was less certain the man had been sent up for the right reason.

"What if I told you Tommy lied about where he was that night?" Nathan said softly. "Would you come then?"

Jack stared out across the street. He could feel a pulse start to pound in his temple. "What you're really saying is that *you* lied about that night."

"I had to. He threatened to hurt someone I cared about if I didn't."

"What are you talking about?"

"Do you remember my cousin Olive? She and my aunt came to live with us after my uncle died."

Jack skimmed his memory, summoning up a hazy image of a slight redhead with glasses. "Vaguely."

"You probably didn't even notice her, but she used to follow me around all the time. I think she just needed someone to pay attention to her. Tommy didn't come right out and say it, but he let me know if I didn't swear to the police he was at my house all night, something bad might happen to Olive."

"I take it he wasn't at your house."

"He slept over just like we said, but I woke up during the night and found him gone."

"And you never once thought about going to the police? Or to your father? He was a big shot in the county. He could have protected you from Tommy Driscoll or anyone else who threatened you."

"I wasn't worried about myself. My only concern was Olive." Nathan's voice dropped. "Poor kid was already a mess. She took her dad's death hard and I wanted to protect her. She was so fragile that even an empty threat could have pushed her over the edge. But I didn't think Tommy's threat was empty. He had a cruel streak, Jack. You never saw it because he kept it hidden from you. But not from me. I was often the brunt of it."

"You never said anything."

"I guess growing up with my old man, I got used to dealing with bullies."

Don't, Jack thought bitterly. *Don't let him get to you. None of this matters anymore.*

So what if Nathan had lied about Tommy's whereabouts? Jack had never been charged. He'd left town a free man and he'd put all that behind him. He was happy here in Houston. Or at least, content. He had friends, a good job. Why go digging up the past now?

Because a man had been sent to prison for a crime he may not have committed. Wayne Foukes was an arsonist, a drug dealer and a serial rapist who'd left a string of ruined lives in his wake. He deserved to be incarcerated, but so did Anna's killer.

"Will you come?" Nathan pressed.

"What is it you expect me to do?"

"What you do in every other place with a corrupt police department. Expose the dirt so we can clean it up."

"You don't think people will question my presence in a town where I haven't set foot in over fifteen years?"

"You have the perfect excuse for coming back. You need to settle your uncle's estate. You can even stay in the cabin while you decide what you want to do with it. I'll have someone go in and give it a good cleaning, stock the refrigerator. You might even enjoy a few days on the lake. All I'm asking is that you keep your eyes and ears open while you're here. Ask a few discreet questions. You'll know how best to handle the situation once you get here."

"I'll think about it," Jack said.

"For how long?"

Irritation flared. "For as long as I need to. I have a job. I can't pick up and leave whenever I want."

"Don't take too long," Nathan warned. "Whatever you decide, I would appreciate you keeping this call between us. My life could depend on it."

He knew how to end the conversation on a dramatic note. Jack would give him that.

Slipping the phone in his pocket, he leaned a shoulder against the building as he mulled over his options. He had vacation time coming. He was between assignments and he'd caught up on all his paperwork. There would never be a better time to take a few days off. Still, he wasn't about to rush into anything. He needed to have a drink, relax, sleep on it. Then he'd talk things over with his boss on Monday.

He deliberately turned his thoughts to more pleasant options, like how to spend the rest of his Friday evening. He could go across the street to Lola's and have a drink with the other Blackthorn employees who would already be congregating in the shadowy back room for happy hour. Like Jack, they were mostly former law enforcement—cops, FBI, DEA. They all got on well except for the military contingent, the ex-Special Forces teams that were often deployed overseas as private security. Mercenaries. Those guys kept to themselves.

He decided he wasn't in the mood for a raucous celebration so he thought about heading over to Ninfa's on Navigation for solo margaritas and fajitas. But it was a popular eatery and on a Friday night with the Astros in town, chances were good he'd need a reservation. He chose a third option. Home.

His apartment was several blocks away, but he didn't mind the rain. Dodging umbrellas, he merged with the pedestrians hurrying toward bus stops and parking garages. The theater crowd would soon converge, tying up traffic for blocks. He was glad to be on foot.

As he strode along the sidewalk, the back of his neck tingled. He could easily chalk up the sensation to imagination or the residue of an unsettling conversation, but Jack had learned a long time ago to listen to his instincts. To pay attention to the signs. He was being followed.

He searched the mirrored facade of the building across the street and turned very casually to observe

the traffic. Nothing seemed amiss, but in the chaos
of rush hour, a tail could be hard to spot.

OLIVE BELMONT HURRIED along the shadowy streets,
suppressing the desire to glance over her shoulder
as she rounded the corner toward home. She'd had
a funny feeling all day that something was wrong,
though she tried to tell herself it was nerves.

School would start in another three weeks and
this would be Olive's first term as principal at Pine
Lake High School. Just shy of thirty, she was the
youngest to ever hold the position and she knew the
school board would watch her every move, waiting
to pounce on any misstep. With that kind of pressure, she was allowed a few jitters.

Her unease was more than first-day butterflies,
though. Pine Lake wasn't the town it once was.
Maybe it had never been the idyllic hamlet she'd always thought it, but now the community seemed on
the verge of losing itself to the same pandemic of
drugs and malaise that affected hundreds of rural
towns across the South.

The decline had been gradual in Pine Lake. So
slow that only lately had Olive noticed the deterio-
ration. But on a sultry evening like this, one could
almost smell the rot. Even the beautiful old Queen
Anne homes along Primrose Avenue had fallen into
a sorry state and it seemed to Olive that every other
week she saw at least one U-Haul heading out of
town. She wondered if that was why she'd been of-

fered the job as principal. Maybe no one else had wanted the position.

With all the added stress came the nightmares, those terrifying falling dreams from her early teens. The situation was always the same. She found herself on a bridge clinging to the edge for dear life. She could feel her fingers slip as her legs flailed helplessly. Then she was falling backward into a misty abyss as a shadowy figure peered down at her from the guardrail. Olive could never see a face, but she thought the watcher might be her dad. He'd been killed on a bridge when his car and another had collided head on.

Olive had gone years without having that dream, but for weeks now the recurring nightmare had plagued her sleep. She never hit the water, but on at least two occasions, the sensation of falling had been so real that she'd awakened to find herself on her knees in bed, clutching the headboard. The smell of pine needles and swamp had permeated her tiny bedroom, though she knew the scent was nothing more than a lingering effect from her dream.

She hoped the nightmares would go away once school started and she settled into her new position. Meanwhile, a chat with Mona Sutton might help. The guidance counselor had been a lifesaver when Olive had been a new student at Pine Lake High School fifteen years ago. Armed with a doctorate in psychology and a fierce determination to save the world, Mona Sutton had taken Olive under her wing, helping her through the pain and loneliness and seemingly insurmountable guilt over her father's tragic death. Olive's mother had been too lost in her own grief to notice that her fourteen-year-old daughter was quietly having a nervous breakdown. Mona had stepped in, then and years later when the pressure of college had caused the dreams to resurface. She would help again if need be, but their relationship might be trickier now that Olive was her boss.

Olive's tiny bungalow was just ahead on the corner of Elm and Holly. As she approached the intersection, she finally gave into her premonition and glanced over her shoulder. It was still early, but not a soul stirred. Even the eateries along East Market Street had already closed their doors for the evening.

An abandoned air had settled over the town, deepening Olive's unease. For a moment, she had the terrifying notion that everyone had packed up and left Pine Lake while she'd been working late, readying herself for the coming school year. But she wasn't completely alone. A dog barked from a fenced backyard and she could hear the idling of a car engine somewhere nearby.

As she stepped off the curb, headlights flashed on, catching her in the face. She froze like a deer, staring wide-eyed into the bright beams until she heard the engine rev and then she instinctively retreated to the sidewalk. A split second later, a dark sedan sped past her. She didn't recognize car or driver nor did she get a look at the license plate. The car was going too fast. Reckless driving wasn't unusual in Pine Lake where drag racing down Main Street on a Friday night was still a popular pastime. But she wasn't on Main Street and Olive could have sworn the car had deliberately swerved in her direction as it zoomed past her.

She stood underneath a streetlight, heart thudding as she tried to rationalize the incident. Someone had probably recognized her and decided to have a little fun at the expense of the new principal. She was a small woman and looked years younger than her age so there would be more of the same once school started. No doubt a steady stream of challenges to her authority. She'd better buck up and learn to hide her nerves if she had any hope of making it through the first semester, let alone the whole school year.

Wiping clammy hands down the sides of her pants, she looked both ways and then hurried across the street to her house. She let herself in and then turned the lock behind her. Dragging over a footstool, she shot home a bolt at the top of the door, a precaution she hoped was unnecessary.

It was an unusual place for a lock. Designed to keep someone in rather than a dangerous element out.

JACK HAD DECIDED to stop off at a corner bar where he could watch the street. One drink had somehow turned into three and by the time he left, traffic had thinned and darkness was falling. He headed for the shower as soon as he got home, standing for a long time under the steamy water as he tried to banish the barrage of unwanted memories that had kept him drinking at the bar.

Anna's face swam up out of the back of his mind. He wanted to remember her the way she'd been the summer he fell in love with her, a gorgeous brunette with a killer smile and legs that went on forever. Instead, he kept seeing her dragged from the lake, lips blue, skin gray, eyes glazed and sightless.

Senior year was supposed to have been their time, a long goodbye before college took them in separate directions. Jack had been elected captain of the football team; Anna had been the head cheerleader. They were the all-American cliché. In hindsight, even her death seemed banal, the most beautiful girl in school meeting a violent and untimely demise. The news offered up similar tragedies on a daily basis, but for whatever reason, Anna's story had captivated the national media.

For a while, Jack hadn't been able to leave his house without cameras being shoved in his face. His picture had been splashed across tabloids and gossip-style news programs, making him the most hated seventeen-year-old in the country. And then one night, Wayne Foukes had been pulled over for a broken taillight. Among the cache of drugs in his trunk, the police had discovered Anna's missing class ring.

Once Foukes was charged, the reporters disappeared, but the people Jack had known his whole life continued to avoid him. It was almost as if they needed to believe him guilty in order to justify their behavior. He'd left town vowing never to return, but now Nathan's phone call had changed everything.

Dragging on a pair of jeans, he ambled into the kitchen to scour the refrigerator for dinner. Pickings were slim. He settled on a beer. Later, he'd order in. Watch a movie, crash on the couch. Assuming he'd be able to sleep.

The night stretched before him, empty and endless. He turned on the Astros game to fill the quiet as he glanced aimlessly around his apartment. The small space, sleek and minimally furnished, boasted a view of the Houston skyline, but it had never felt much like home. Turning up the volume, he took his beer out to the balcony to enjoy the night air. The rain was coming down harder now and he held his hand over the railing to collect a fistful of water.

He could hear his cell ringing inside and he told himself to ignore it even as he flicked the water from his fingers and stepped back through the door. He picked up the phone from the counter and glanced at the screen. It was a Pine Lake prefix but the number wasn't Nathan's. Or at least not the number of the phone he'd called from before.

Jack carried the phone back out to the balcony with him. "Jack King."

"Hello, Jack King. Tommy Driscoll calling." He gave a low chuckle. "Man, oh, man. I wish I could see your face right now. I must be about the last person you expected to hear from tonight."

Pretty damn close. What were the chances he'd hear from his two former best friends on the same night? Jack wasn't a big believer in coincidences. Something was up. He tried to brace himself, but Tommy Driscoll's voice took him aback. He sounded exactly the way Jack remembered—loud, jovial, a man always up for a good time. Except now the jollity sounded forced, but maybe Jack's perception had been tainted by time and Nathan's innuendoes. Or maybe Tommy Driscoll had never been the easygoing guy Jack had thought him.

"What can I do for you, Tommy? Or should I call you Sheriff Driscoll?"

"You heard about that, did you?" He sounded pleased. "Back in our glory days, who would have ever thought a pair of hell-raisers like us would turn out to be cops?"

"I'm not a cop."

"You were, though. Houston PD. See? I've kept up with you through the years." He paused as if expecting Jack to say the same about him. "Now you're with that outfit I see on the news. The Blackthorn Agency. You guys go into some hairy places from what I hear. Must be exciting. Good money, too, I bet. You've done all right for yourself, seems like."

In spite of everything, Jack thought. "Why are you calling, Tommy?"

"I need a favor, buddy. It's about Nathan."

Jack was instantly on alert. "What about him?"

"Have you heard from him lately?"

Something in Tommy's voice prickled Jack's scalp. "Why would you think I'd hear from Nathan? You guys cut me loose a long time ago."

"You sound bitter," Tommy said.

"No, just careful."

"Can't say as I blame you, considering the way you were treated. We were all just scared kids back then. I'm not making excuses, but it was a rough time for everyone."

Sure sounded like he was making excuses. And the half-hearted apology was only now being extended because Tommy needed something from Jack. Just like Nathan did. He wasn't about to make it easy on either of them.

"This is awkward as hell," Tommy muttered into the loaded silence. "I can't imagine how strange it must be for you."

"No, you can't."

Tommy drew in a sharp breath as if his anger had been goaded. Then he said in a strained voice, "Look, man, I wouldn't even be bothering you except I think Nathan may be in some trouble. Serious trouble. And now that it's all coming home to roost, he's looking for a way out."

"What do you mean?"

Tommy hesitated. "I think he may be trying to set me up."

"For what?"

"I haven't figured that out yet."

Jack stared out into the night, dotted with street-lights spanning the misty cityscape, but his mind had already traveled deep into the piney woods of East Texas. "What is it you expect me to do about it?"

"Nothing, buddy. Not a damn thing. That's the whole point of this call. If Nathan tries to get in touch, I'd appreciate a heads-up. Otherwise, go on about your business."

"You still haven't told me why you think he'd try to get in touch with me."

"He's desperate. And he and your uncle were tight. Maybe he thinks you still have a score to settle and he can somehow use it to his advantage. A word of advice from an old friend." Any hint of joviality disappeared from Tommy Driscoll's voice. "Don't believe a word that comes out of his mouth. Nathan Bolt is a pathological liar. Always has been. Just like his old man."

"What has he lied about?" Jack asked carefully.

Tommy hesitated. "Maybe it doesn't even matter anymore."

"Maybe it does," Jack said. "What did Nathan lie about?"

Another pause. "He wasn't home the night Anna was killed. He left before midnight and didn't come back until nearly sunrise."

Chapter Two

Jack sat on his uncle's boat dock as a fine mist settled over the lake. All around him, the landscape was eerie and primal, a swampy labyrinth of channels and bayous that stretched all the way across the Louisiana border. The town of Pine Lake was less than a quarter of a mile away, but the woods blocked the lights. He could see nothing but the silhouette of trees and a glimpse now and then of the old lake bridge through the curtains of Spanish moss hanging from a dense forest of bald cypress.

Damn, it was dark out here.

Jack had forgotten what it was like to be that deep in the country, without the glow of skyscrapers to create a false daylight. As he stared out at the water, the night came alive. A loon trilled from the woods as a mosquito buzzed his ear. A female alligator grunted nearby, warning predators away from her nest. The nocturnal sounds stirred an uneasy excitement. *You shouldn't have come back here*, a voice in his head taunted. *You're asking for trouble.*

Yeah, maybe he was.

He hadn't told anyone he was coming. Not Nathan, not Tommy. But the cabin had been spotless when he arrived, the cupboards and refrigerator well stocked. Even his uncle's fishing boat had been scrubbed and gassed up. Jack wasn't too pleased by the preparations. Nathan's overconfidence bugged him, but it wasn't misplaced. He was here, wasn't he?

All weekend long he'd brooded about those two phone calls and then come Monday morning, he'd headed upstairs to talk things over with his boss, Ezra Blackthorn. The taciturn head of the agency had listened carefully to Jack's story, but he hadn't offered much in the way of advice. Wading back into the muck of his past had been Jack's decision alone. As much as he dreaded what he might find, he couldn't ignore any chance, no matter how slim, of finally bringing Anna's killer to justice. To resolve once and for all what had really happened on that long-ago Friday night.

But he had no delusions about easy answers. His investigation was likely to get messy. He didn't trust Nathan or Tommy to tell him the truth. Obviously, they were each working an angle. He could well imagine Tommy Driscoll getting involved in something shady. Even as a kid, Tommy's innate charm and athletic prowess had fostered a sense of entitlement. He'd learned early on that he could talk his way out of anything and Jack doubted his attitude had changed now that he wore a badge.

Nathan was a little harder to figure out. He already had money and prestige. Why risk his standing in the community?

Jack really didn't care what either of them was up to. He did care that one or both had lied about their whereabouts on the night of Anna's murder.

He watched the water with a pensive frown, unable to shake his disquiet. His mind had strayed to such a dark place that when he saw a light flicker on the old lake bridge, he half convinced himself he was being paranoid.

But no, there it was again. Not a flickering light as he'd first thought, but the bobbing beam of a flashlight moving across the wooden deck. The bridge had been abandoned decades ago, but the rotting floorboards and creaking beams had never dissuaded the local daredevils. He watched for a moment, thinking back to his own misadventures on that bridge.

The light was no longer moving, he noted. The beam stayed stationary for so long that he had to conclude someone had set the flashlight down on the deck or perhaps wedged it between the braces. If he concentrated hard enough, he could almost conjure a form standing at the guardrail. He was tempted to start up his uncle's boat and train the spotlight on the bridge, but even so powerful a beam would be swallowed by the misty darkness. Besides which, this was none of his business. He hadn't come to Pine Lake to get sidetracked—

He heard a splash as something heavy hit the

water. Then the flashlight beam swept down and over the lake, glimmering sporadically through the trees. Jack was far enough away that he couldn't be spotted, but he instinctively shrank back into the shadows.

For the longest time, the light moved slowly over the water. Then the glow vanished, only to reappear bobbing toward the end of the bridge. A few minutes later, Jack heard the sound of a car engine on the far side of the lake. Not a frantic rev but a stealthy purr as the car slowly drove away on the old dirt road.

He didn't know what to make of the splash or the light. People had been known to use the lake as a dumping site. If caught, the offense carried a stiff penalty, but back in Jack's day, the area around the bridge had rarely been patrolled. Which was undoubtedly the reason Anna's killer had chosen to dump her body from the deck.

That splash…

What were the chances another body had been thrown from the bridge on the very night he'd returned to Pine Lake? Slim to none, Jack decided, but he knew the sound would niggle at him all night. Might as well take the boat out and have a look.

A FEW MINUTES LATER, Jack maneuvered away from the dock and headed into the channel. It was even darker on the water. He didn't want to turn on his running lights, much less the spotlight in case someone lurked nearby. But it was dangerous to be on the lake blind. Dangerous for others, dangerous for him. If he strayed from the middle of the channel, he had to worry about cypress knees below the surface and those thick mats of aquatic vegetation that could entangle the boat's propeller.

He turned on the spotlight, keeping the beam concentrated on the water ahead of him. As he neared the bridge, he shifted into neutral and drifted as he trained the light along the banks where ground mist thickened. Cypress trees rose from the shallows like bearded sentinels, obscuring both ends of the bridge. Beyond the lake was the pine forest and all along the water's edge, a creeping carpet of lily pads and lotus.

He made a pass underneath the first span of the bridge, once again searching along the banks and in the deeper water of the channel before returning through the second span. Clouds blocked the moon so thoroughly he had to rely solely on the spotlight. Even through the mist, he could pick out turtles and frogs and the red glowing eyes of an alligator, but he saw nothing unusual in the water.

If someone had thrown a body off the bridge, they would have more than likely weighted it. It could take days or even weeks to surface. He was wasting his time and he knew it. All he'd heard was a distant splash. All he'd seen was a bobbing flashlight. He had no reason to believe that anything untoward—

She was there in the shallows, floating on her back among the lily pads.

Jack used the trolling motor to navigate through

the strangling vegetation and then a paddle to hold the boat steady as he observed the body. He didn't attempt to drag her from the water. She was dead and had been the moment the bullet passed through the back of her skull and exited between her eyes. During his time as a cop, he'd seen that jagged, X-shaped wound before, usually in drug-related executions. The facial damage was extensive, but the best Jack could tell, she was young, probably no more than early twenties, with long blond hair floating all around her.

He sat for a moment, awash in memories before he took out his phone and called Tommy Driscoll's number.

The phone rang five times before Tommy finally answered. He sounded annoyed and winded. "Driscoll."

"Tommy, it's Jack King."

"Jack? It's a little late, isn't it, buddy?"

"Not for this."

"You heard from Nathan?" he asked anxiously.

"I'm calling about something else."

A long silence. "Where are you?"

"Sitting in my uncle's boat on Pine Lake. I'm about fifty yards south of the old bridge. You'd better get out here. There's a body in the water."

He heard the sharp intake of Tommy's breath. "Do you know who it is?"

"Female Caucasian. Blonde, slim build from what I can tell. She's young. Early twenties, I'm guessing.

Looks like someone shot her in the back of the head and then dumped her body off the bridge."

"No need for an ambulance, I take it." Tommy's voice seemed oddly hushed.

"No, but you'd better send for the coroner. I'll stay with her until you get here."

"Jack?"

"Yeah?"

"What are you doing on Pine Lake?"

"I don't think that much matters right now, does it?"

"It might," Tommy said. "I'll see you in a few minutes. We'll talk then."

Jack dropped the phone back in his pocket, his gaze still on the body. He cut the spotlight. The garish brilliance somehow seemed offensive. As darkness slid over him, he had the uncanny feeling that he wasn't alone. He told himself it was just the situation. The similarities to Anna were bound to unnerve him. But he couldn't shake the notion that someone was near. Someone watched him.

Turning on the spotlight, he raked the powerful beam all along the banks and then into the shadowy corners of the bridge. He almost expected to see someone at the guardrail staring down at him. No one was there. He was alone on the water with the dead woman.

He made one more sweep, this time slanting the beam up in the trees. As he shifted the light, he caught a glimpse of something white through the cypress branches. A barn owl, he thought, or a snowy egret. But as he focused the light, he realized the shimmer of white wasn't in a tree, but at the very top of the bridge. For a moment he could have sworn someone was up in the rafters.

He shook his head and moved the light away. Crazy notion.

He sat in the gently rocking boat and let the night sounds settle over him. Then he angled the beam back to the truss. The white object was still up there.

Pushing off with the paddle he let the boat float back into the center of the channel before he started the motor. The outboard hummed throatily as he navigated toward the bridge. Backing off the throttle he aimed the light up through the Spanish moss. Whatever he expected to find was not what he saw. Never in a million years could he have imagined such a sight.

The floor of the bridge was a good fifteen feet above the water and from the deck, a series of braces and struts climbed another twenty feet to the iron beam that ran the length of the bridge.

On top of that narrow girder, a woman lay curled in the fetal position.

OLIVE'S EYES FLEW OPEN. She had been dreaming again about falling. Down, down, down into that misty abyss. The nightmare had been so real that she still had the smell of the swamp in her nostrils. She could even feel a breeze on her face.

She lay for a moment, breathing deeply as she tried to calm her racing heart.

What was that creaking sound? She couldn't place it. The ceiling fan, maybe?

"Don't move," a male voice said nearby.

That brought her fully awake. She started to sit up, but a hand on her shoulder eased her back down and she realized another hand had clamped around her wrist. Panic exploded. Her instinct was to lash out at the intruder, to fight him off with every ounce of strength she could muster, but she was suddenly aware of her surroundings. That creak didn't come from any ceiling fan. She wasn't even in her bedroom. She was—

"Where am I?" she gasped, as her whole world tilted.

"Don't worry. I've got you." The voice was deep and silky smooth. Olive found it at once soothing and terrifying.

"Got me…where?"

"You know the old bridge over Pine Lake?"

"Yes, I know it…" She trailed away as she tried to peer through the darkness. A light glimmered somewhere below her. She felt compelled to turn and stare into the beam, but the swaying sensation and the hand on her shoulder kept her immobile. "I'm on the bridge?"

"More or less," the voice said.

Terror surged as she pictured the gaping holes in the rotting floorboards and the unstable framework towering over her. The image dizzied her and she had to suppress the urge to flail her arms, searching for a handhold.

Now she understood the creaking and swaying.

"You have to stay calm, okay? I'm not going to let you fall, but you need to do exactly as I say."

"Fall?" She started to tremble.

"We're going to get you down, but it'll take some maneuvering."

"Why can't I just stand up and walk off the bridge?" she asked in a quivering voice.

"You're not exactly on the bridge. You're on top of it."

"On top of it?"

"On top of the truss."

"That's impossible." But even as she protested, she realized the feathery forms all around her were the tops of cypress trees. She could feel the night air on her face and the hardness of the support beneath her. The nightmarish sensation of falling gripped her again and she said in a terrified whisper, "Please don't let go of me."

"I won't," he promised.

Somehow she believed him. "How did I get up here?"

"You tell me."

"Sometimes I sleepwalk. I have these falling dreams—"

"You're not going to fall. If you go, I go and I'm not in the mood for a swim. So here's what I need you to do. Right now, you're lying on your left side facing out toward the water. Take a moment to get your bearings."

"I can see cypress trees. There's a light somewhere below us—"

"Don't look down. Stay focused on the task at hand. Listen to me carefully. I need you to roll to your stomach, but there's not a lot of space to operate. I'd say about a foot, give or take."

She put out a hand and felt nothing but air. "I can't. There isn't enough room."

"If there's room enough for you to curl up and sleep, there's enough room for you to roll over. Besides, you're small. You don't need much space."

"I can't. Please don't make me."

He was silent for a moment. "What's your name?"

"Olive Belmont."

"Olive? As in Nathan Bolt's cousin?" He sounded surprised.

"Yes. You know Nathan?"

"We go back. Listen to me, Olive. We're going to do this together, okay? I'm right here with you. You'll be able to see me in a moment. Put your right hand on the support and clamp your fingers around the edge. Do the same with your left as you slowly position yourself facedown."

Olive clutched the edge, but she didn't roll over. Not for the longest time. Then drawing a breath, she slowly shifted her body. The rafter rocked and the whole frame seemed to shimmy. She froze. "I can't."

"Yes, you can. This bridge isn't going anywhere. Just take your time. That's it. Nice and easy."

Olive tried to ignore the metallic screeches and the disorienting sway of the structure beneath her. Instead, she let that soothing voice guide her as she maneuvered her hands and body until she lay face down on the support, still breathing hard and trembling.

"Good job. Now you're going to get on your hands and knees and slowly crawl toward me. Got it?"

"Yes."

"Don't look down, look at me. Whenever you're ready."

Olive rose on hands and knees, balancing herself on the precarious beam. The light from below provided enough illumination so that she could see the silhouette of the man facing her.

"Follow me, Olive. Nice and slow. We're in no hurry. We have all night."

His voice flowed over her, so honeyed, so comforting in the dark. She could see the gleam of his eyes, the curve of his jaw. He seemed very steady on the rafter. Not the least bit afraid.

She drew a deep breath and released it. "I'm ready."

They began to move slowly, inch by inch toward the end of the bridge. He had the more difficult job because he was maneuvering backward on the unsteady support. He didn't look over his shoulder or down at the water. He kept his eyes trained on Olive.

She tried to do the same. She didn't dare look out over the lake. She didn't dare peer down into that misty abyss.

"Almost there. You're doing great, but I need you to stay focused, okay? I need you to stay calm." He came to a halt and she did the same. His eyes gleamed in the dark as he held her gaze. "Now comes the tricky part."

"The tricky part?" she echoed faintly.

"We're going to lower ourselves over the side. The braces form a sort of ladder at the end of the horizontal beam. I imagine that's how you got up here."

"I don't remember."

"It's not as hard as it sounds. I climbed this thing more times than I could count as a kid. Nathan did, too."

"That doesn't sound like Nathan," she said.

"It took a lot of double-dog daring."

She heard a smile in his voice and shivered. "I'm ready."

He went over the side first, finding his footing and then clinging with one hand as he waited for her. Olive counted to ten and then eased into position, lowering her legs and grappling for a foothold. The movement must have put too much pressure on the rusty bolts. She heard a loud snap and then one end of the beam dropped out from under her. For one heart-stopping moment, she found herself in a free fall.

Then a hand clamped around her wrist. "Easy now. I've got you."

"Don't let go!" she pleaded.

"Not a chance," he said as he tightened his grip.

Chapter Three

He pulled her up to the ladder and then his arm came around her, holding her close as she found her footing. Now that one end of the beam had popped free, the integrity of the structure was even more compromised. The struts clanged ominously as Olive and her rescuer began their descent. At deck level, he climbed over the guardrail and helped her through. She clutched his arm, mindful of all those missing planks and the glisten of water far below.

"Let's get off this thing," he said and took her hand, leading her from the bridge. When they were safely on the bank, she stopped and bent double, catching her breath.

"Are you okay?"

She drew in air. "I just need a moment."

"You did great," he said.

She sucked in several more breaths before she straightened. She could see him more clearly now. He was tall and slim with broad shoulders and long legs. Dark hair, dark eyes. Tantalizingly familiar.

She could see him so well, in fact, she wondered if the moon was up, but then she realized the light came from a bobbing boat at the edge of the water.

"I don't know how I can ever thank you. If you hadn't found me when you did…" She trailed off on another shudder. "How did you even know to look for me up there?"

"I didn't. It was just a lucky break." He paused. "You really don't remember how you got up there?"

"I don't even know how I got to the lake. I have no memory of leaving my house." She glanced down at her bare feet, realizing for the first time that she was in her pajamas. The fabric was summer-weight cotton. Sheer if the light hit her just right, but modesty was the least of her worries. She pulled a leaf from her hair and watched it swirl to the ground. "I don't remember anything."

"What about sounds?" he asked. "Did you hear any loud noises? A car engine maybe?"

She shook her head. "I don't think so. But sleepwalking occurs in deep sleep. I never remember anything."

He stared down at her for a moment. "Do you do this often?"

"No, not in years. I had a sleep disorder in my early teens, but I thought I'd outgrown it. Anyway, the point is, it's like having amnesia. I don't even know what awakened me."

"Maybe you sensed my presence up there on the

beam or felt my hand on your shoulder. I did my best not to startle you."

"Thank you. That could have been disastrous for both of us." Now that she was on solid ground and the danger was over she found herself growing curious about him. He still seemed familiar and very capable. "You said you and Nathan go back. Did you go to school together?"

"From kindergarten on."

"Wait. I know you," she blurted as recognition dawned. "You're Jack King."

She saw a frown fleet across his face. "My reputation precedes me, I guess."

"It isn't that. I remember you from the year my mother and I moved to Pine Lake. We stayed with Nathan and his dad until we got our own place. You used to come by the house with Tommy Driscoll and some of the other seniors. You'd hang out by the pool. I was invisible to most of Nathan's friends, but you were always nice to me."

"Was I?"

She gave an awkward laugh. "I guess I was invisible to you, too. You don't remember me, do you?"

"I do now, but you've changed. No glasses, no braces." He canted his head, peering down at her in the light. "I think I can still see some freckles, though."

A thrill chased up Olive's spine at his scrutiny. She'd never told anyone—had barely admitted it even to herself—that she'd had a crush on Jack King that year. Nathan's other friends were rude and boisterous, but Jack was different. To a hopelessly romantic fourteen-year-old, he'd seemed deep and introspective. And devastatingly handsome. "You haven't changed a bit," she said.

"I'd wait for better lighting to make that assessment."

"I can see you just fine."

Car engines sounded on the road. Doors slammed and male voices carried in the dark.

"That'll be the sheriff." Jack turned toward the trees and called out to the newcomers. "Down here!"

Olive scanned the woods anxiously. "You called the police? Why didn't you wait for their help to get me down?"

"I didn't think it a good idea to leave you up there any longer than was necessary. Besides, I didn't call the cops because of you." He hesitated, his eyes going past her to the water. "No easy way to say this. I found a body in the lake before I saw you on the bridge."

Olive's hand crept to her throat. "A body?"

"A woman."

"Do you know who she is?"

"No. But if she's local, the sheriff or one of his deputies can likely identify her."

Olive closed her eyes in dread. "If she's local, she's probably someone I know." A former student perhaps or even a friend. "Pine Lake is small. Everyone knows everyone."

"I remember."

She turned to the lake in horror. Someone she knew could be out there in the water at that very moment, dead and drifting. It gave her the oddest feeling. Part fear, part sadness, part relief. If she'd fallen from the rafters, she'd likely be dead and drifting, too.

But she was safe and sound thanks to Jack King and this night was no longer about her.

She wrapped her arms around her middle. "Could you tell how she died? Was it a drowning accident?"

His gaze on her deepened. Olive shivered at the intensity of his stare. The scruff on his lower face made him look dangerously enigmatic. The way he towered over her made him seem just plain dangerous.

"You should wait and ask the sheriff those questions. I wouldn't want to be accused of interfering in his investigation."

"Of course. I understand. It's just…what if it *is* someone I know?"

"You'll find out soon enough," he said with a nod as Tommy Driscoll and two of his deputies came crashing through the underbrush. The subordinates wore uniforms, but Tommy had on jeans, cowboy boots and a white dress shirt with pearl buttons. He looked as if he had been out dancing. Or up to no good.

He stopped dead when he spotted them. Then he

said something over his shoulder to one of the deputies before he joined Olive and Jack on the bank.

Olive tried not to show her disdain for the Caddo County sheriff. She respected his position but not so much the man. If Jack King had been her favorite of Nathan's friends, Tommy Driscoll had been her least. Even as a teenager, he'd been arrogant and overbearing and she'd seen no evidence of evolution.

Unlike Jack, the years hadn't been kind to him physically. His muscles had softened as his features had hardened. He was still married to his high school sweetheart, but rumors about affairs had run rampant for years. Beth Driscoll taught science at Pine Lake High School. She was a lovely woman and a dedicated teacher. Olive would never understand why someone who had so much going for her would put up with a man like Tommy.

He and Jack eyed each other warily before Tommy gave a brief nod. "Jack."

"Tommy."

They didn't shake hands, Olive noted.

"Good to see you, buddy. Sorry it has to be under these circumstances. When did you get into town?"

"A few hours ago."

"Helluva homecoming." Tommy's gaze slid to Olive, taking in her pajamas and bare feet. "Olive? What are you doing down here?"

"She just got here," Jack said.

Tommy frowned. "Got here from where?"

"From the road. She said she heard my boat."

It was all Olive could do not to turn and gape at Jack. Somehow she managed to stifle her shock under Tommy's narrow-eyed inspection.

"Let's let Olive answer for herself," he said.

She nodded. "I was out for a walk when I heard the boat. I came down here to see who was out on the lake so late. I thought someone might be dumping trash. You know what an environmental hazard that poses."

"I know you like your causes," Tommy said. "But you're telling me you were out for a walk at this hour? In your pajamas? Without shoes?"

"I didn't expect to end up so far from the house. I've been under a lot of stress lately and I only meant to get a bit of fresh air to clear my head. Next thing I knew, I'd walked all the way to the lake."

Tommy's gaze went from Olive to Jack and then back to Olive. He lowered his voice as he took a step toward her. "Are you sure you're okay?"

His implication couldn't have been plainer and she resented it on Jack's behalf. She told herself it was silly to feel so protective of a stranger, but she found herself pressing closer to him anyway. "Of course, I am," she said coolly. "And I think you've more important things to worry about than me."

He gave her another curious look before turning back to Jack. "Where's the body?"

Jack gestured toward the lake. "I can take you out in the boat and show you."

Tommy nodded. "Yeah, let's go have a look."

The deputies still hovered a few feet away and Tommy went over to confer for a moment.

"What was that all about?" Olive whispered furiously.

"Trust me, I know what I'm doing," Jack said.

"By lying to the police?"

"It'll be okay," he assured her.

Olive wasn't as convinced, but it was a little too late for second thoughts. Not only had she gone along with Jack's fabrication, she'd embellished his account. If she came clean now, it would make both of them look foolish and possibly suspect.

But those lies had flowed just a little too easily, from her and from Jack. Olive had never considered herself the subversive type, although as Tommy had pointed out, she supported causes near and dear to her heart and had never been shy about voicing an opinion. Deliberately misleading the police, though? That was a serious matter and one she shouldn't have undertaken so lightly.

She watched nervously as the two men climbed into the boat and pushed off. When they'd cleared the bank, Jack started the engine and steered them across the channel to the shallow water on the other side. They sat with the motor idling as he angled the spotlight down through the lily pads.

It seemed to Olive they stayed out on the water for an awfully long time. What were they talking about?

Finally, they headed back. Jack tied off and they disembarked.

Tommy climbed up the bank to where Olive and the two deputies waited. "Be easier to get her out from the other side," he said. "Hope you boys brought your waders."

Jack came up the bank, too, and she found herself instinctively gravitating to his side even as she kept her focus on the sheriff. "Who is she, Tommy?"

He hesitated. "I guess you'll find out soon enough. It's Jamie Butaud."

Olive felt sick. "Are you sure?"

"Pretty certain. The physical description matches up. And Jack here spotted a tattoo on her left arm. I remember seeing it on Jamie."

"A mermaid," Olive murmured.

"You knew her?" Jack inquired gently.

"She was in one of my classes a few years ago before she dropped out of school. I always worried about her. She seemed so lost."

"She worked for Nathan, didn't she?" Tommy asked.

Both men peered at Olive in the dark, but it was the fierceness of Jack's sudden concentration that took her by surprise. "Yes, as a receptionist."

"When was the last time you saw her?" Tommy asked.

Olive shrugged. "I don't remember specifically. I rarely go to Nathan's office, but I would see Jamie in town from time to time, usually with her boyfriend."

"She was still seeing the Waller kid?"

"Marc? Yes, as far as I know."

"Bad news, that boy. Comes from a long line of bad news." Tommy ran a hand through his hair. "Look, here, you two. I need you to keep quiet about this, at least until we can notify next of kin. And I'd like the chance to speak with Waller before he tries to skip town."

Olive glanced from Tommy to Jack. "You don't think her death was an accident, do you?"

"That's safe to assume," Tommy said. "We'll know more after the autopsy, but the first thing we have to do is get her out of the water. You don't need to be here for that. I'll have Hank run you home while we wait for the coroner."

"I can take her," Jack said.

Tommy didn't look too pleased by the offer. "In your boat? How's that going to work? Olive lives in town, last I heard."

"We'll go to my uncle's cabin and get my car. Seems to me you'll need all your manpower here, Sheriff."

Tommy scowled down at her. "You okay with that arrangement, Olive?"

She resisted the urge to inform him that she'd much rather be alone with Jack King than any of the other men present. Instead, she nodded and turned to Jack. "Thanks."

"No problem."

Tommy was still frowning. "I'll need to see each

of you in my office first thing in the morning. And remember what I said about keeping this quiet."

Jack took Olive's arm and helped her navigate the slippery bank. Once they'd cast off, she averted her gaze from the spot where he'd taken Tommy to view the body. But she couldn't help glancing back at the bridge. She let her gaze travel up the iron braces to the very top of the truss. If Jack hadn't spotted her… if he hadn't climbed up there beside her…

Something came to Olive as the bridge receded in the distance. Now she understood why Jack had asked her if she'd heard a loud noise or a car engine.

In all likelihood, she'd been asleep on that beam when Jamie Butaud's killer had thrown her body off the bridge.

A LITTLE WHILE later Jack pulled his car into Olive's driveway and parked. She'd been very quiet on the ride into town, staring out the window until she needed to give him directions to her house.

"Are you okay?" he asked.

"Yes, just lost in thought." Her voice had taken on a raspy edge, either from nerves or the night air.

Jack cut the engine and the headlights went out, but the street lamp on the corner cast a hazy glow inside the car. Her skin looked pale in that light, but her face was alive with color—the copper of her freckles and the bright blue of her eyes framed by the deep russet of her hair. She peered at him so steadily he had to shift his gaze to the window, instinctively taking stock of their surroundings.

She lived on a quiet street in the oldest part of town. The houses on her block were small with wide front porches and tidy fenced yards. Jack had grown up only a few blocks over in a sturdy old Craftsman that his mother had loved. It had pained her to leave the house of her dreams, but after everything that had happened to their family, Pine Lake no longer seemed like home.

"What an awful homecoming you've had," Olive murmured, echoing his thoughts. "This night must bring back a lot of bad memories for you."

"This town is nothing but a bad memory." He glanced in the rearview mirror, scanning the street behind them.

"If you really feel that way, why did you come back?"

"My uncle's estate has some loose ends that can't be tied up over the phone or in an email."

"Oh, of course. I was so sorry to hear about his passing. He was a nice man. I always enjoyed his stories." Her regret sounded deep and genuine.

Jack turned in surprise. "His stories?"

"He took classes at the community college where I sometimes teach at night. He was one of my favorite students."

Jack stared at her in astonishment. "Leon went to night school? I never knew him to be interested in anything but fishing."

"Then it may surprise you to learn that your uncle was a very gifted writer."

He cast her a doubtful glance. "Are you sure we're talking about the same Leon King?"

She smiled. "Yes, same man. He always spoke highly of you. He was very proud of the way you'd turned things around after everything you went through." She paused thoughtfully. "For the record, I never believed you did it."

"Why?"

His blunt challenge seemed to catch her off guard, but she recovered quickly. "Because of the way you would look at Anna. Anyone could see you were crazy about her. And why wouldn't you be? She was a beautiful girl, inside and out."

"She was," he said quietly.

"And because it wasn't in you. You weren't capable of hurting anyone. I doubt you are now unless someone backs you into a corner."

"You deduced all that in the space of one car ride?"

"I deduced all that a long time ago. You're a good guy. Just like your uncle. Why else would you have climbed to the top of that bridge to rescue me?"

Her conviction caught *him* off guard. When Jack had decided to come back to Pine Lake, he'd braced himself for the whispers and gossip. The lingering suspicions. But he hadn't prepared himself for Olive Belmont.

"I've been away from here for a long time," he said. "I may not be the man you think I am."

"I may not be the woman you think I am," she countered. "If you think about me at all," she added sheepishly.

"Hard to forget someone you meet on top of a bridge."

He saw a shiver go through her as she turned to stare out the windshield. She looked very enticing with her hair all mussed and her lips slightly parted. Another time, another place and Jack might have responded to the subtle invitation in her smile. But a hookup was the last thing he needed, particularly with Nathan Bolt's cousin. He'd come to town to poke a hornet's nest. Depending on what he found, things could get ugly. Sides might have to be chosen. After all was said and done, he'd return to Houston while Olive would still have to live here. Jack knew only too well what it was like to be a pariah in Pine Lake.

She gave him another tentative smile and he tamped down the urge to tuck back her hair as he studied her face in the dim light.

"I know now why you told the sheriff I had just arrived at the lake," she said. "I figured it out in the boat. You think I was on top of the bridge when the killer dumped Jamie's body in the water."

"Seems a safe bet. It couldn't have taken more than five minutes for me to get to the bridge after I first heard a splash and you were already up there."

"So you wanted to place me on the road rather than the bridge."

He shifted his position, turning toward her as he relaxed his arm across the back of her seat. "I heard that splash and then a few minutes later, a car engine. The vehicle drove away on the other side of the lake. Even if you really had been on the road at the same time the body was dumped from the bridge, you wouldn't have seen anything."

She gave him an anxious look. "That explains why you asked if I'd heard a car engine. But I told you before—I never remember anything when I sleepwalk."

"Jamie's killer wouldn't know that, though. He or she might not want to take the chance that something would eventually come back to you."

That gave her pause. She cast an uneasy glance over her shoulder. "Do you really think I could be in danger?"

He wanted to reassure her that all would be well, but a false sense of security was never a good idea. She needed to watch her back. They weren't out of the woods yet. The story they'd concocted for Tommy Driscoll was only a little more plausible than the actual truth. "As long as we don't give the killer a reason to feel threatened, he'll lay low. As far as anyone knows, I was the first to arrive on the scene. If he gets skittish, he'll come after me."

"That doesn't give me much comfort," she said with a frown.

"It should. I know how to handle myself."

"Leon told me that you'd been a cop. And now you're some sort of security consultant. With all your experience, you must have some idea of how Jamie died."

"Are you sure you want to know?"

She swallowed. "I wasn't. But now I think you have to tell me."

"She has what appears to be a large exit wound between her eyes. I'm guessing she was shot at close range in the back of the head."

"In the back of the head…" Olive repeated numbly.

"Without a closer examination of the body or a look at the autopsy report, I can only speculate. But I've seen the pattern of the wound before in execution-style murders."

"Execution?" She stared at him in shock. "Who would do such a thing to poor Jamie?"

"You never heard talk about her involvement in any illegal activities?"

"She got into some trouble when she was younger. Drugs. Possession, I think. Her mother asked Nathan to represent her, but the family didn't have any money. He agreed to take the case pro bono if Jamie agreed to go to night school and get her GED."

"What about her boyfriend?"

"I don't know him personally, but Tommy was right. Marc Waller is bad news. He was also arrested for possession but with the intent to sell. If convicted, he could have gone to prison for a very long time. But

Nathan got the case dismissed because of an unlawful search. Needless to say, that didn't go over well with local law enforcement."

"Nathan Bolt seems to be the go-to attorney for drug charges," Jack observed.

"Well, there aren't a lot of choices in the area and my cousin is very good at what he does." She sighed. "The news about Jamie will devastate him. If it turns out that Marc Waller had anything to do with her death, Nathan will never forgive himself."

These revelations were all very interesting to Jack. On the night of his return, he'd stumbled across a murder victim who happened to be a young woman that Nathan Bolt had taken under his wing. The timing was a little more than Jack could swallow as happenstance.

"It's late," Olive said. "And we're both expected at the police station first thing in the morning so…"

"Right. I'll walk you to the door."

"You don't need to do that. I'm fine."

Jack reached for the door handle. "For my own peace of mind, I'd like to have a look around before I go."

"To be honest, it's probably best for my peace of mind, too."

They got out of the car and walked up the porch steps together. The front door stood ajar and Olive turned to him with a worried frown.

"I'm sure it's nothing. I probably failed to close it earlier."

Jack brushed past her, glancing over his shoulder to scan the street and all the shadowy corners of the yard before toeing open the door. "Where's the light switch?"

"To your left."

"Wait here." He eased through the quiet house, giving each room a thorough search before returning to the foyer. "All clear."

"Thanks for checking." Olive stepped inside and followed his gaze to the bolt at the top of the door. "A precaution. Not that it did any good tonight."

"You unlocked the deadbolt in your sleep?"

"Apparently."

"You should get a security system, one with a loud enough alarm to wake you if a door or window is opened."

"Yes, my mother had one put in when the episodes first started. As I said, I thought I'd outgrown them, but after tonight, I won't take any chances. I'll arrange for an installation as soon as possible."

Jack took a last sweep of the small, but comfortable living area. The walls were white and the furniture gray, not unlike the nondescript color scheme in his apartment. But Olive had punctuated the space with pillows and throw rugs in bright shades of red and turquoise. He observed everything, not because her design aesthetic interested him, but because a house could reveal a lot about the person who lived there.

Olive Belmont seemed to be an open book. If her cousin was involved in something as shady as

Tommy had implied, Jack doubted she knew anything about it. But then, he had been fooled before.

He stepped out on the porch and scoured the darkness. The breeze had picked up, fluttering through the trees in Olive's front yard and unleashing the scent of jasmine from the bushes that grew up her fence. It was all very lush and homey and familiar and yet Jack felt strangely unmoored as if coming back here to his hometown had caused him to lose his bearings.

He turned back to Olive. "Are you sure you'll be all right for the rest of the night?"

"I'll be fine. If I sleep at all, it won't be deeply enough to leave my bed."

An image of that bed floated through Jack's head—crisp white linens and soft, soft pillows.

"Well, good night, then." He bent impulsively to kiss her cheek. The action took both of them by surprise and she jerked her head just enough so that his mouth brushed hers.

He didn't pull away or offer an apology. Instead, he tangled his fingers in her hair and brought his mouth to hers, this time on purpose. She responded by parting her lips and kissing him back. When he pulled away, she looked disoriented, as if she had just awakened from another harrowing adventure.

"What a strange night this has been," she murmured.

"Hasn't it, though?" he said over his shoulder as he strode down the steps.

Chapter Four

Olive was just coming out of the local coffee shop the next morning when she spotted Jack on his way in. He held the door for her and she stepped out on the sidewalk to join him, taking a moment to discreetly admire the fit of his faded jeans and the cotton shirt that he wore untucked and rolled up at the sleeves.

His hair was even darker than she remembered, his eyes a deep, rich chocolate. Despite what she'd said the night before, he had most definitely changed since their high school years. The harsh light of day emphasized the fine lines around his eyes, the resolved set of his jaw and a chiseled chin. The changes didn't so much age him as harden him. He was a man in his prime rather than the seventeen-year-old boy who had been driven out of town by both his elders and his peers.

"Good morning," she said in a tone far too bright for the circumstances. "Looks like we had the same idea."

"It would seem so." He stood with one hand still on the door as he gave her a long assessment.

His scrutiny was only fair, she supposed, since she'd done the same to him. Still, she was secretly relieved that she'd taken time with her appearance even though the sleeveless white dress and caged heels were for work and not for Jack King. Normally, she wouldn't have been so formally turned out during summer break, but she had a faculty meeting later that morning, the first of the new school year, and she wanted to make a good impression. That Jack seemed to appreciate her fine-tuning was merely icing on the cake.

"Are you headed over to the sheriff's office?" he asked.

"I've already been in." They moved away from the door to the edge of the street so as not to block customer traffic. "We spoke briefly. I really couldn't add much to my previous statement and Tommy revealed very little about the investigation. Although I gather word has already gotten out about Jamie's death. That's not surprising. Secrets are hard to keep in a town this small."

"That hasn't been my experience." His tone was enigmatic. "You repeated what you'd already told him last night?"

"I stuck to our story if that's what you mean." She shot a quick glance over her shoulder and then leaned in. "Lying to the police before breakfast, let alone my first cup of coffee, is a lot more stressful than I would have imagined. I don't know how career criminals do it."

"If it makes you feel any better, you ad-libbed like a champ last night."

She winced. "That doesn't make me feel better. Worse, in fact. I work with kids. I take my responsibility as a role model very seriously. What does it say about my character that I could so easily withhold the truth in a murder investigation?"

"You have every right to protect yourself. Nothing you could have told him would change the course of his investigation. You didn't see or hear anything. Why put yourself needlessly at risk?"

"I guess."

He glanced back at the shop door. "I should grab my coffee and go. Tommy will be expecting me."

"And I need to get to work. Good luck with your interview." She paused. "Should we get together later to compare notes? I have a meeting at ten, but I'll be in my office all afternoon."

"I'll try to give you a call."

A noncommittal answer if Olive had ever heard one, but she decided not to take it personally. She'd enjoyed their good-night kiss—had been quite stunned by it, in fact—but she didn't attach too much importance to the gesture. Jack had acted on impulse and she'd responded in kind. Blame it on the lingering adrenaline from her rescue. Olive freely acknowledged an attraction to him, but really, wasn't his allure little more than an old memory?

Besides, it was probably for the best to keep some distance. After last night, there would undoubtedly be talk. Olive wasn't one to live her life in fear of gossip, but like it or not, reputation mattered in a small town, especially for someone in her position. The next few weeks were crucial. They could well set the tone for the whole school year, if not the rest of her career. She would be foolish to invite distraction and controversy when everything she'd worked so hard for was at stake.

She murmured a goodbye and then turned to cross the street only to have Jack grab her arm and yank her back to the curb as a black pickup truck roared through the intersection. Her heel caught in a crack and she went down in an ungainly sprawl. The coffee cup flew out of her hand, exploding on impact with the pavement. Mortified, Olive could only stare helplessly at the spreading brown splotches on her white dress.

Jack was instantly at her side. "You okay?"

"I think so." She took his hand and quickly scrambled to her feet. A small group had already started to gather and Olive would have liked nothing more than to sink right through the sidewalk.

"You sure you're okay?"

"Yes, fine." She dusted her hands and tried to salvage her poise. If anything could be more embarrassing than taking a spill in public, it was doing so in the presence of a high school crush. "That's the second time you've had to come to my rescue in as many days. And the second time in less than a week that

I almost got hit stepping off a curb. I really should pay more attention."

"That driver was going way too fast. Brazenly speeding right down Main Street." He retrieved the cup and tossed it in a nearby trash bin.

Olive's ankle ached and the heel on her right shoe wobbled. The morning had turned disastrous. Now she would have to go all the way back home and change, leaving little time to prepare for her meeting. She lamented the turn of events until she reminded herself of Jamie Butaud's fate and the kind of morning that awaited her family and friends. Put in the proper perspective, a coffee-stained dress and a battered shoe were hardly worth fretting over.

"Did you get a look at the driver?" Jack asked her.

"It happened too quickly. What about you?"

"I was able to get a partial plate number. I'll give that and a description of the vehicle to the sheriff. Someone is bound to recognize that truck." He scanned the crowd for a moment before zeroing back in on her. "You said this had happened before?"

"Last Friday night. I worked late and it was already dark by the time I left for home. A car came out of nowhere and the headlights blinded me as I stepped off the curb."

His voice sharpened. "Last Friday night?"

"Yes, why?"

He hesitated. "Nothing. I was just thinking back to my own Friday night. Same vehicle?"

"No, it was a car then. A dark sedan, but I couldn't

tell the make or model. I really don't think it's anything to worry about. I have a feeling I'm being tested."

"What do you mean, tested?"

The intensity of his focus caught Olive off guard and unease crept over her. Why did she suddenly have the feeling that there was much more to Jack King and his return than he had previously been willing to acknowledge? Despite their history, he was a stranger and now she couldn't help but wonder why he had really come back to Pine Lake. Something was going on, with him and with this town. At that moment, her decision to keep a safe distance seemed like a very good idea.

"In three weeks, I'll be starting my first semester as principal of Pine Lake High School," she explained.

He lifted a brow. "Principal?"

She gave a shaky laugh. "Please don't say I look too young for the job. I've already heard that too many times as it is."

"I was about to say, you're a lot braver than I am."

"We'll soon see, I suppose. Anyway, I think these incidents are challenges to my authority. A way to intimidate me. Neither vehicle came close to hitting me."

Jack's expression sobered. "That's a pretty dangerous way to intimidate. You could have been seriously injured when you fell. Whatever the motive, they shouldn't be allowed to get away with it."

She started to put a restraining hand on his arm, but dropped it to her side instead. "They're just kids. As soon as they accept that I can't be scared off, they'll move on." She glanced around. A few bystanders still huddled nearby as they whispered furiously among themselves. Evidently, Jack had been recognized and Olive's heart sank. Word would spread across town like wildfire now. Jack King had come back to Pine Lake on the same night a young woman had been murdered. And Olive Belmont had been seen with him at the lake and now in front of the coffee shop. No telling what her role would become once the game of telephone took hold.

Jack had noticed the crowd, too. It would be hard to miss the whispers and open stares.

"Ignore them," she said.

He gave a low laugh. "These people mean nothing to me."

His derision sent a chill through her, almost as frigid as the sudden frost in his eyes. "Then why come back here?"

"I told you last night—loose ends."

"But those loose ends don't really have anything to do with your uncle's estate, do they? I saw the way you looked at that crowd just now. *These people.* Why do I have a feeling you've come back for revenge?"

"There's a difference between justice and vengeance."

Olive's heart thudded in trepidation. The disquiet

she'd been experiencing for days seemed to culminate in his icy stare. "Your uncle never believed that Wayne Foukes killed Anna. I take it you don't, either."

Even as he hesitated to answer, his gaze on her was relentless. "Wayne Foukes is guilty of a lot of terrible crimes, but he didn't kill Anna."

"How can you be so sure unless—"

His voice grew even colder. "Unless I killed her?"

"Unless you have new evidence. I told you last night I never thought you did it."

"You also told me that you think I'm a good guy. The look on your face right now tells me otherwise."

Olive wasn't quite sure how to respond. It was true, she did feel differently about him this morning. He seemed a little too dark and distant, a little too secretive for her peace of mind. But what if he was right? What if Anna's murderer had gone free all these years and was still living in Pine Lake? Still attending Sunday morning church services and Friday night football games? What if the killer was an acquaintance or a friend or even someone she had dated? What if a cold-blooded murderer had lain low all these years, hidden among the populace of a small, insular town, only to resurface and kill again fifteen years later?

Jack waited patiently for her to respond.

She tried to subdue her agitation as she gave him an honest answer. "I still think you're a good guy.

But a good guy on a mission can cause an awful lot of trouble."

"The innocent have nothing to fear from me."

She suspected his was also an honest answer, but it only served to deepen her foreboding. Because in that moment of candor, Olive had glimpsed something in his face that she hadn't witnessed before. Beneath his cool, steady persona was a simmering anger that took her breath away. Despite what he said about justice and vengeance, there was no mistaking his intent. Jack King meant to have his pound of flesh.

She closed her eyes on a shiver. The town wouldn't even see it coming. A few discreet questions and suddenly suspicions would flare and bad feelings would fester. Neighbor would side-eye neighbor. Olive couldn't fault him for wanting justice or even revenge for the way he'd been treated, but she dreaded getting caught in the fallout.

His gaze was still on her, a singular focus that drew another shiver. She tried to look away, but his stare was too hypnotic. Why hadn't she seen this coming? Even on top of the bridge, even in the throes of terror, instinct should have warned her that she was in the presence of a very dangerous man. Her instincts were warning her now. Screaming at her, in fact.

"I…should go," she said.

Before she could step away, he reached out and tucked back an errant strand of hair that had fallen loose from her ponytail. Her pulse jumped at even so slight a touch and Olive knew she was in real trouble.

"Watch where you're going," he said.

"Good advice." *Such* good advice.

JACK GLANCED OVER his shoulder to where Tommy Driscoll sat behind his desk. The Caddo County sheriff was on the phone and had been for a full five minutes.

When he caught Jack's eye, he palmed the mouthpiece. "Sorry about this."

"No problem."

"You need anything? Cup of coffee…bottle of water…"

"I'm good," Jack said as he turned back to the window. "Take your time."

He was glad to have a few minutes to collect his thoughts. With an effort, he unclenched his fists and relaxed his fingers as he tried to rein in his emotions. But even now, he could feel the surge of an unexpected anger.

Jack had been in control for so long he'd forgotten what it was like to give in to those latent resentments. The fury that had defined his behavior all through college had eventually given way to the bitter resignation of his twenties and finally to the jaded disdain that had kept him restless and distrustful at thirty-three. His earlier anger had blindsided him. That the townspeople and their lingering suspicions could still goad him back into that dark place didn't bode well for an objective investigation.

Being back inside the police station didn't help. On the morning he'd first learned of Anna's death, Jack had been ushered into this very office. Despite the passage of time, he still remembered those hours vividly—his mother's tremulous voice waking him from a deep sleep. His grogginess as he dressed and staggered down the back stairs to the kitchen where his father and Sheriff Brannigan sat drinking coffee. His father's somber expression. The lawman's grim tone. *Son, I need you and your folks to come down to the station with me.*

Jack had found out about Anna on the ride downtown. Then later, in the throes of grief and shock and flanked by his parents, he'd sat across the desk from Brannigan for his first interview. The questions had seemed innocuous at first. When had he last seen Anna? What time had he dropped her off? Had they argued that evening?

From there the interrogation had progressed to the most intimate details of their relationship.

Were the two of you sexually active?

Yes, sir.

For how long?

A few months.

Did you have intercourse last night?

Yes, sir.

But didn't you say you took her home because she wasn't feeling well?

Yes. That's true.

But she felt well enough to have sex with you?

I...guess so.

Tell the truth, son. Did you pressure that girl? Use a little force when she wouldn't give in?

No, sir. It was her idea.

Her idea? She asked you to take her home early because she was sick and then she asked you to have sex with her in your car? I find that a little hard to believe. Especially since her folks swear they never heard her come in. Her bed wasn't slept in last night. How do you account for that?

I can't.

Truth is, you didn't take her home, did you, Jack?

I swear I did! I walked her to the door and I waited until she was inside the house before I drove off.

You know what I think? I think you were all hopped up on adrenaline after the football game last night. You guys won, right? You scored the winning touchdown. You must have been in the mood to celebrate. Yeah, you were raring to go and things got a little rough, maybe. Things got out of hand and Anna ended up dead.

That's a lie! I would never hurt Anna!

Or maybe she wouldn't give you what you wanted and so you decided to take it. Hotshot like you always gets what he wants. You're a real popular guy, aren't you, Jack? Not used to hearing no, I bet. When Anna fought back, you bashed her in the head with a rock.

*No! That's not what happened. You have to be-
lieve me—*

*Then you tore off her clothes and had your way
with her.*

Please—

Made you feel pretty powerful, didn't it?

Please, I'm going to be sick—

*I'm sick, too, Jack. Sick all the way down to my
soul at what you did to that poor girl.*

I didn't do anything. I swear—

*Go ahead and cry if you have to, but those tears
won't help when we match your DNA to the sample
we took from Anna's body.*

Please stop. Please. I can't take this anymore—

*You didn't stop when Anna begged you to, did
you? Afterward you panicked. You had to finish her
off and so you strangled her. You threw her body off
the old Pine Lake Bridge and then you went home,
crawled into your comfortable bed and went to sleep.
Did I get it right, Jack? Tell me where I'm going
wrong.*

*You're wrong about everything! I didn't do this.
Mom. Dad. Tell him. Please. I could never do something like this—*

*Your mom and dad can't help you, son. But I can.
Tell me what really happened last night. Tell me the
truth and I swear to God I'll do everything in my
power to help you through this.*

Jack's parents had lived in Pine Lake for most
of their lives. Sheriff Brannigan was a friend. They

were of the mind that if Jack cooperated, if he simply told the truth, everything would be all right. Five hours into the intense grilling, Jack's father had finally excused himself to go call a lawyer.

When they were allowed to leave the police station, word had already spread about Anna's murder. A crowd had gathered in the parking lot. Friends, neighbors, classmates. The open suspicion and outright name calling had been hard enough to take, but nothing had gotten to Jack quite like his mother's silent weeping. She'd taken to her bed as soon as they got home while his father had gone about the grim business of figuring out how to pay for the attorney. Throughout the whole ordeal, they'd stood by him, never for a second letting on that they doubted his innocence. But after that morning, it seemed to Jack they'd never quite looked at him in the same way again.

"JACK? YOU READY, BUDDY?"

Tommy's drawl pierced through the barrage of memories and Jack turned from the window with a scowl. "What?"

"The interview. You ready?"

"Yeah, let's get it over with."

Tommy stretched. "Sorry again for the interruption. The mayor tends to get a little long-winded when he's on a tear. I don't answer to him, but I try to lend a sympathetic ear now and then. Anyway, before he called, you were telling me about a black pickup truck that nearly ran Olive over this morning."

"Yeah, it came pretty damn close."

"Black trucks are a dime a dozen around here. Could be hard to track down even with a partial plate. Do you remember any identifying marks? Bumper stickers? A dented fender or a cracked windshield, maybe?"

Jack folded his arms and leaned a shoulder against the window frame. "The paint job was flat black. Custom."

"That'll help." Tommy jotted down a few more notes, tore the sheet from the pad and went out to the squad room where he handed the paper to an officer. He returned a moment later carrying two mugs of black coffee. "You look like you could use a caffeine jolt. I know I can."

Jack had forgone coffee earlier after the incident with Olive. Now, though, he accepted the cup gratefully and took a tentative sip. "Damn."

Tommy chuckled. "Around here, we like it strong enough to put hair on your chest."

"Mission accomplished." Jack went over to the desk and placed his cup on the corner as his gaze traveled across the rows of framed photographs and citations on the walls. "Are all those commendations yours?"

Tommy looked pleased that he had noticed. "I've had a good run."

"It would appear that you have."

He motioned Jack to a seat and then went around the desk and sat down heavily in his creaking chair. "About that black truck." He took a quick sip of his coffee. "Clearly a case of reckless driving, but you're not thinking the driver *deliberately* tried to run Olive down, are you?"

"She said it was the second time she's almost been hit in less than a week. She thinks she's being tested because of her new job."

"Sounds about right. Kids around here drive like bats out of hell. You and I were no different back in the day. And just between us, Olive Belmont isn't the most observant pedestrian. She walks around town with her head in the clouds half the time. Not just her. I've seen people on their cell phones step into the street without ever looking up. Then add in the texting drivers and you start to get a real grim picture."

"Olive wasn't on her phone."

"No, but she was talking to you, right? She was distracted. I'm not saying I won't look into it. I will. But even if I manage to track down the truck, all I can do is give the driver a good talking to. Sometimes that's enough."

"I appreciate your efforts," Jack said. "I wouldn't want anyone to get hurt."

"Nor would I. But right now I've got bigger fish to fry with this murder investigation." Tommy settled back in his chair and clasped his hands behind his head. His casual demeanor didn't fool Jack. Sheriff Brannigan had seemed amiable, too, at first, but he'd quickly revealed himself to be ruthless and obsessed. A simple and single-minded investigator who couldn't be bothered to look for other suspects because Jack had fit his profile. Only months later when he'd failed to come up with anything more than circumstantial evidence had an ex-con in the area pinged his radar. Jack had wondered more than once about the coincidence and convenience of that traffic stop. Wayne Foukes's arrest had taken the pressure off a beleaguered county sheriff. From that day forward, Brannigan had run uncontested every four years until his retirement.

"I need to hear about last night," Tommy was saying. "Start at the beginning and walk me through everything that happened up until the time my deputies and I arrived on the scene."

Jack told him about spotting the flashlight beam on the bridge, hearing a splash and then moments later, the sound of a car driving away.

"So you decided to take the boat out and investigate," Tommy said.

"Don't tell me you wouldn't have done the same."

"Probably," he admitted. "How long did it take you to locate the body?"

"Not long with the spotlight. Five or ten minutes."

"What did you do once you found her?"

"I called it in. Then I tied off the boat and waited on the bank so that I could flag you down when you arrived."

"And that's when Olive came along?"

"Yeah, a few minutes later."

"You didn't think it strange to see her wandering around in the dark in her pajamas?"

"I've seen stranger things."

"Still, the behavior seems peculiar even for Olive."

"You heard what she said. She thought someone might be dumping trash in the lake. I guess she wanted to catch them red-handed."

Tommy gave him a pensive scowl. "Did you know she used to be a sleepwalker?"

Jack shrugged. "She seemed wide awake when I spoke to her."

"That's the thing, though. You can't always tell."

"Have you seen her sleepwalk?" Jack asked.

"Not in years. But when she and her mother were first staying with the Bolts, Nathan and I once found her outside in the middle of the night, sitting cross-legged in the front yard staring out at the street. When I waved my hand in front of her face, she didn't even blink. It was eerie as hell. Another time Nathan said she was out all night before anyone noticed her missing. Next day, she didn't remember a thing. It was like it never happened."

"Okay, so she used to sleepwalk," Jack said. "Like I said, she seemed awake and lucid when I talked to her last night."

Tommy picked up a pencil and examined the eraser. "You didn't get a look at the vehicle that drove off?"

"It was long gone before I arrived at the bridge.

And there's no way Olive could have seen it from the road."

"That's pretty much what she said."

Jack shrugged. "Then I guess we're done here."

"Not quite."

Jack had started to rise, but he sat back down as Tommy leaned forward, his gaze narrowed and suddenly hostile.

Jack's guard came up. "What else can I do for you, sheriff?"

"You can tell me what you're doing in Pine Lake."

"I'm here to put my uncle's affairs in order."

Tommy didn't appear convinced. "Let me put it another way. Why have you come back now? Leon passed away months ago. Are you sure there's not another reason for your sudden trip down memory lane? I told you the other night, I've kept up with your career. I know what you do at the Blackthorn Agency. The thought has crossed my mind that someone might have hired you to investigate this office."

"Is there a reason someone would want this office investigated?" Jack countered, taking a perverse satisfaction in Tommy's apparent discomfort.

"Someone's always got a beef. Comes with the territory. But you and me—" Tension crackled as he leveled his gaze across the desk at Jack. "We'll have a real problem if I find out you're working for Nathan Bolt."

"I'm not working for anybody. I'm here of my

own accord." Now it was Jack who leaned forward. "But you're right. There is another reason for my trip. Did you really expect I would do nothing about the bombshell you dropped the other night?"

"I was hoping you were smart enough to leave that alone, buddy."

"Then why tell me about it at all if you didn't want me to come to Pine Lake?"

"I wanted to warn you about Nathan. I needed to make you realize how untrustworthy he is."

"See, that's the part I still don't get," Jack said. "What made you think Nathan would contact me in the first place?"

Tommy glanced toward the squad room. The door was closed but he lowered his voice anyway. "One of my informants told me that Nathan's been asking a lot of questions about this office. I was told flat out that he's looking to hire an outside investigator to take me down. And since he and your uncle were so tight, it stood to reason he'd try to get you on his side."

"His side?"

"There's a war going on in this town, Jack. Things have changed since you lived here. Used to be all we had to worry about was a few penny-ante pushers operating out of the old Shady Grove Apartments. The kind of product we're seeing nowadays makes Pine Lake seem like a border town. I've suspected for a long time there's a local kingpin, someone with enough smarts and clout to cover his tracks.

Someone who instills the kind of fear or loyalty that keeps his people from cutting deals when they get arrested."

"Are you saying that person is Nathan Bolt?"

Tommy shot another glance toward the squad room. "I'm not prepared to go there yet, but he's involved at some level. We make a bust, nine times out of ten the first person the perp calls is Nathan."

"He's a good attorney from what I hear."

"Yeah, but he's not the only lawyer in the county or even in Pine Lake. And he's sure as hell not the cheapest. You have to wonder who's paying him and why."

"Just because he caters to a certain clientele doesn't make him a criminal." Jack played devil's advocate even though he'd had the same thought about Nathan last night. "He comes from money. Why would he risk his reputation, let alone his freedom, by getting involved in something so potentially dangerous?"

"He has money by Pine Lake standards, but not the kind it takes to finance a political campaign. He's always been ambitious. You know that even better than I do. Remember back in school? His competitiveness bordered on obsessive. He was always looking for an advantage, always looking to come out on top. He's had his eye on Austin for years."

"Even more reason to keep his nose clean," Jack said.

"Not if he's thought this through and Nathan is

nothing if not shrewd. You were smarter but he was the more conniving. Think about it. He hires himself out to the drug trade just long enough to salt away the money he needs to launch a respectable state senate campaign. Now he's ready to walk away, but questions are being asked. Dots are being connected. And maybe some of his people aren't quite as loyal as he thought."

"People like Jamie Butaud?"

Tommy's eyes flashed. "What do you know about Jamie?"

"You said last night she worked for Nathan. Wouldn't be the first time a police informant met with a violent end."

"I'm not going to speculate about suspects and motives with you," he said with a pompous edge. "What I will say is that I put very little past Nathan Bolt. If he thought this office was closing in on him, he'd do everything in his power to taint the process. Plant some rumors, plant some evidence and then bring in an outside investigator to put it all together. Masterminding the takedown of a corrupt county sheriff's office would be a pretty effective way to launch a political career."

"Is this office corrupt?" Jack asked bluntly.

"My men and I aren't perfect, but there's not a dirty cop among us."

Jack glanced up at the framed citations. He didn't take the awards or Tommy's declaration at face value. Even as a teenager, Tommy Driscoll had been given to excesses and shortcuts. Now, in his early thirties, the slight paunch and sagging jawline spoke to a lack of discipline. Jack could well believe the man dirty. But had he ever been capable of murder?

"Where were you the night Anna was killed?" he asked suddenly.

Tommy sat in stunned silence before he erupted. "What the *hell*, Jack?"

"It's a simple question. Logical after what you told me on the phone. Why not answer if you've nothing to hide?"

The chair squealed ominously as Tommy shot forward. "Because I don't answer to you. And I sure as hell don't appreciate the implication."

"There's no implication," Jack said with a shrug. "Just a question. You've admitted that you lied about Nathan's whereabouts. So why not tell me where you were?"

"Exactly where I said I was."

"At Nathan's house. All night long."

"Damn straight."

"But now that you've taken Nathan out of the picture, it's just your word."

Tommy was silent for a long moment. "Where are you going with this?"

"Maybe I just want to know why my two best friends lied about their whereabouts on the night my girlfriend was murdered."

"It won't change anything."

Bitterness crept into Jack's voice. "Maybe not, but I think the very least you owe me is the truth."

Tommy's mouth thinned. "What is it you want to know?"

"Where did Nathan claim he went that night?"

"He said he was out looking for Olive. He said she was sleepwalking again. He noticed that her bed was empty and he went out to find her."

"And you believed him?"

"I had no reason not to at the time. I didn't know then what a liar he was and I'd seen Olive sleepwalk for myself."

"Why didn't you tell any of this to the cops?"

"It didn't seem like a big deal. Who knew the police would come down so hard on you? I wanted to help out a friend, that's all. And as for Olive, she'd already been through hell with her dad dying and having to relocate to a new town. It seemed best for everyone to just keep quiet."

"Or did you keep quiet because placing Nathan at home all night gave *you* an alibi?"

"Why would I need an alibi? I didn't kill Anna."

"Neither did I, but that didn't keep me from being a suspect."

Tommy hesitated, as if having to hold his temper in check. "You're looking for closure and I get that. But you're never going to find all the answers. Anna left the house after you dropped her off. Maybe she went out to meet someone or maybe she went for a walk. We'll never know. It was nothing more than very bad luck that Wayne Foukes happened to be in the area that night." He paused once more. "You want everything tied up with a nice, neat bow, but that's just not going to happen, buddy."

"Maybe not," Jack said. "But we do know one thing for certain. Wayne Foukes didn't kill Jamie Butaud."

Chapter Five

Olive stood at her second-story office window staring down at the campus. The benches and courtyards were empty but soon enough the common spaces would teem with activity. The classrooms would fill up and the parking lot would overflow onto the empty field across the street. There would be fisticuffs to break up, punishments to dole out and irate parents to soothe. One crisis after another.

Pine Lake had always been a rowdy school, but right now the building seemed eerily silent. Olive had to fight the compulsion to glance over her shoulder. The hollow hallways seemed haunted by the ghosts of Jamie Butaud, Anna Grayson and all the other students that had been lost over the years. Olive had never thought her imagination overactive, but earlier when she'd returned from lunch, she could have sworn she heard phantom footsteps in the stairwell.

The faculty meeting had gone so well that she had no reason for the creeping disquiet. She knew most of the staff, had worked with them for the past six years. If anyone resented her appointment, they'd managed to swallow their pride and conceal their disapproval for the sake of an agreeable work environment. So why did she still feel so anxious? Why the sensation of falling when she was wide awake and on solid footing?

Olive wanted to believe the close call with the truck and the whispering townspeople had rattled her or maybe she was experiencing a sort of PTSD from the terrifying incident on top of the bridge. Not to mention the murder of a young woman who had once been her student and the less-than-forthcoming statement Olive had given to the police. Except for the scare with the dark sedan, all of those events had happened after Jack's return. She didn't blame him for any of them. She certainly didn't think him a killer. But already he'd wreaked havoc on her equilibrium. Already he'd unnerved and jolted her, and now she couldn't shake the notion that she was perched precariously at the edge of a very high cliff.

"Olive?"

She turned from the window with a start. Mona Sutton stood in the doorway, head slightly cocked as she gave Olive a quizzical look. "Are you okay?"

Olive mustered a smile. "Don't I look okay?"

"In my experience, looks can be deceiving. I had to call your name three times before you heard me."

"Sorry. I have a lot on my mind these days. And I thought everyone else had gone home."

Mona hovered in the doorway. "May I?"

"Yes, of course. Come in." Olive motioned her to a chair as she took a seat behind her desk.

"You're making this space your own, I see." Mona's gaze skimmed the artwork on the walls and the framed diplomas and certificates that hung over the credenza.

"Trying to." Olive kept a picture of her dad on her desk and another shot of her and her mother taken last year on a cruise. Other than the photographs and a potted succulent, her work space remained uncluttered. How long that would last was anyone's guess.

Mona gave another of those assessing looks. Olive straightened and tried to present a placid demeanor, but from their first meeting fifteen years ago, the guidance counselor had always been able to read her a little too well for comfort. And yet despite all the intimate details she'd gleaned from Olive's life over the years, Mona Sutton remained a closed book. Beyond her educational and professional credentials, Olive knew very little about the woman's background, though it was obvious she came from money. Her wardrobe alone would cost at least half her yearly salary and then there was the late-model BMW and the restored house on Primrose Avenue.

In her early forties, she was still a very attractive woman—tall, blonde and regal. She could be charming and even funny when she had a mind to be, but she rarely socialized in Pine Lake. As far as Olive could tell, Mona Sutton seemed perfectly content to dedicate herself fully to her career. In addition to her position as guidance counselor, she also had a private practice with a few select clients that she saw in an office in her home.

"I suppose you've heard about Jamie Butaud," she said.

Olive winced. "Such a horrible tragedy. I would have made an announcement at the meeting this morning, but I was instructed by the sheriff not to say anything. Not that it matters. Most everyone in town probably knows more than I do by now."

Mona crossed her legs, displaying the red sole of her high heel. "Instructed by the sheriff, you say. That explains the talk I heard."

"What talk?"

"That you were the one who discovered her body."

Olive said in shock, "What? No, I wasn't. I arrived at the lake after she'd been found. Actually, it was Jack King who discovered the body. Do you remember him? Tall with dark hair and very good-looking."

Mona lifted a brow. "Interesting that you would choose his physical attributes to jog my memory rather than the more obvious tag."

"You mean his relationship with Anna Grayson?" Olive frowned. "That was a long time ago and what happened to him back then doesn't have anything to do with his finding Jamie's body."

"It's curious, though. On the same night he arrives in town, he discovers a body floating in the same lake where his girlfriend's body was found fifteen years ago. A girlfriend he was accused of murdering."

Irritation prickled. "But he didn't kill her. He was

innocent no matter how badly the people in this town wanted to believe otherwise."

"Is that what you think? People wanted to believe him guilty?" Mona was staring at her in that way again.

Olive shrugged. "Maybe not at first. But in their rush to judgment, they treated him so badly the only way to save face was to continue their self-righteous condemnation. They couldn't admit they were wrong because that would have exposed their own character weaknesses. Easier to blame Jack even after another man was tried and convicted."

"Olive Belmont. Champion of the downtrodden."

She pretended to take a bow. "I'll step down off my soapbox now."

Mona was silent for a moment. "You said you arrived after Jamie's body had been discovered. What were you doing at the lake at that hour? And with Jack King, of all people?"

Olive hesitated. Even as a teenager, she'd trusted Mona Sutton with her deepest, darkest misgivings, but the why and how of her lying to the police was a different kind of secret. She'd never before found herself the potential target of a cold-blooded killer.

"I couldn't sleep and went out for a walk. I only meant to take a short stroll to clear my head, but somehow I found myself all the way to the lake."

"Somehow? You don't remember getting there?"

"I just meant that I lost track of time."

"And you happened to run into Jack King?"

"I heard his outboard. I went down to investigate because I thought someone might be dumping trash in the lake. That's when he told me that he'd found a body in the water. He didn't know who she was, of course. It was Tommy Driscoll who identified Jamie from a tattoo."

Mona's voice sharpened. "What tattoo?"

"The mermaid on her arm. It's an unusual design and Jamie was always quite proud of it."

"I remember the tattoo, but I don't understand why he needed it to make—" Mona broke off as realization dawned and her hand crept to her throat. "Oh, no. Was it that bad? I heard she was shot. I just never considered…the damage."

"I don't know if I'm supposed to talk about that," Olive hedged.

"Poor Jamie. She never stood a chance, did she? Deadbeat father, drug-addicted mother. And that boyfriend of hers."

"Marc Waller."

"I certainly hope Tommy—Sheriff Driscoll—is looking into him."

"No doubt he is. A spouse or boyfriend is always a person of interest if not an outright suspect."

"Which brings us back to Jack King." Mona propped an elbow on the chair arm and crooked a finger beneath her chin. "Why do you suppose he's come back here after all this time?"

"His uncle died a few months ago. I expect he has loose ends to tie up."

"Hmm, maybe."

Olive gave her a curious stare. "Why do you think he's come back?"

"Loose ends of one type or another. I always suspected he had issues."

"Anyone would have issues after what he went through." Why did she keep rising to his defense? Olive wondered. Jack King didn't need a champion. He seemed scarily capable of defending himself.

"You're very sympathetic," Mona observed.

"Anyone with a sense of fairness would sympathize with an unjust accusation. Especially when the accused was barely seventeen years old. His whole life was changed that summer."

"You had quite a crush on him, as I recall."

Olive was taken aback. "I never told you that."

Mona smiled. "You didn't have to. I saw the way you looked at him when you passed in the hallway. And all those shy glances from your locker."

The conversation had taken an uncomfortable turn, not because Olive was embarrassed by a typical high school crush, but because it was unsettling to think about being watched from afar. Maybe that was why Mona Sutton was so good at her job. She noticed things no one else did.

"He didn't even know I was alive," Olive said with a self-deprecating smile. "He had eyes only for Anna. They were very much in love."

"*He* certainly was."

A strange little shiver went through Olive at the

emphasized pronoun. "You don't think she loved him?" Then she caught herself. "You don't have to answer that. I'm not even sure we should be talking about this."

"I don't see why not. There's no one here but us. Anna worked for me after school a few days a week, but she was never my client. Even if she were still alive, I wouldn't be violating her confidence by noting that she was a very complicated girl."

"Complicated how?" Olive asked reluctantly.

"She was beautiful, popular, came from a good family. She had all the advantages that poor Jamie Butaud lacked, but there was a side of Anna few people ever saw, including those closest to her. Jack most of all, I suspect."

"What do you mean?"

"She once told me that she would like to follow in my footsteps. I was flattered at first, but I developed serious reservations about her intent. Anna wasn't motivated by a desire to help people. She liked knowing things about them. Secrets. I never gave her my password, but I used to wonder if she'd somehow managed to access my files. It was a feeling I had. And then there was a hacking incident. The whole school system was compromised. Grades were changed, scholarships applications deleted. It would have been an explosive scandal if the administration hadn't managed to keep it quiet. They never found out who did it, but I always suspected Anna was somehow involved."

"That's a very serious charge," Olive said.

"I only bring it up as a cautionary tale. These kids are devious and sophisticated and getting more so every year. Which is why I no longer store my files digitally. I've gone back to the old-fashioned method of hanging folders and locked cabinets. A bored kid with a laptop can be inside the system in a matter of minutes. These days, it takes far more effort to drive to the school and break into the building."

"Point taken," Olive said. "I'll be careful."

Mona smiled and rose leisurely. "I've gossiped too much and taken up far too much of your time. An unseemly pastime for someone in my profession."

"Mona—"

She turned at the door.

Olive wavered, not certain she wanted to bring up her sleepwalking. "We've talked about this before and I think I know the answer. Still, I can't help wondering."

"What is it?" Mona came back into the office and perched a hip on the edge of Olive's desk.

"Back when I used to sleepwalk, I never remembered anything when I woke up. You always told me that amnesia was common."

"It is, especially in children and teens. Less so in adults."

"Really? Why is that?"

Mona settled more comfortably against the desk. "I suspect by now you know more about sleep disorders than I do, but to put it in simple terms, non-

REM sleep has three stages. Stage one is that drowsy, half-awake, half-asleep sensation. Stage two is light sleep and stage three is deep sleep. Children experience amnesia so completely because they spend more time in deep sleep. As you grow older, sleep is more fragmented. You spend more time in the first two stages when the brain is still somewhat cognitive."

Olive conjured an image of herself on top of the old Pine Lake Bridge and suppressed a shiver. She had been up there when Jamie Butaud's killer had thrown her body off the bridge. If a single bit of her brain had still been awake, what might be hidden in her memory?

"If the brain was partially cognitive during a sleepwalking episode and yet the person can't remember the event upon awakening, would there be a way to trigger those memories? Say, through hypnosis?"

Mona shook her head. "Hypnosis would be unreliable at best. Memory is too prone to suggestion and distortion."

"So you wouldn't recommend it?"

"Never for the situation you just described. But I can't help wondering why you're asking."

"No particular reason. I always found it so disconcerting to wake up somewhere other than my bed and have no recall of how I got there. Even glimmers of memory might have helped."

Mona frowned down at her. "You'd tell me if you were sleepwalking again, wouldn't you?"

"You'd be the first person I'd come to if I needed help," Olive dodged. "But other than a few dreams, my sleep is fine."

"The falling dreams again?"

"It's nothing."

"You know from past experience those dreams won't go away until you find the root cause."

Olive smiled. "I know the root cause. I'm afraid of falling on my face as the new principal."

"Sometimes dreams are just that straightforward," Mona agreed. "And sometimes they're like an intriguing puzzle."

JACK SPENT THE rest of the morning at the cabin sorting through some of his uncle's paperwork and belongings, but he could only take so much of the monotony. Restless and bored, he headed back into town for a late lunch and then afterwards, he drove over to Nathan Bolt's office on Commerce Street.

The law firm was housed in a hundred-year-old building that had once been a button factory. The exterior had been painstakingly restored to the original red brick facade and the interior designed to take advantage of the exposed ductwork, beamed ceilings and polished concrete floors. It was the kind of urban setting one might expect to find in Houston or Austin, but the upscale design seemed out of place in a town like Pine Lake.

A well-dressed young woman at the front desk informed Jack that Nathan was in court and not expected back for at least another hour. Could she take his name and number or perhaps schedule an appointment for later in the week? Her demeanor was polite and professional, but she seemed distracted and Jack couldn't help but notice her reddened eyes. The whole office seemed somber and uneasy. Evidently, word of Jamie Butaud's murder had reached her coworkers.

He departed without leaving his name and as he headed across the parking area at the side of the building, he caught a glimpse of a black truck cruising by on the street. He couldn't be certain it was the same vehicle from that morning, but the flat black paint was unusual.

Instead of another reckless display, the driver coasted along as if he were searching for something, almost coming to a stop in front of the law office. Jack watched the truck for a moment before climbing into his own vehicle. He pulled onto the street, trying to keep enough distance not to be spotted. But the truck was going so slowly he found it difficult to maintain the sedate pace without drawing attention.

A few blocks down, a traffic light stopped Jack. While he waited for a green light, the truck picked up speed and disappeared. When the light changed, Jack drove through the intersection, keeping his eyes peeled as traffic became heavier. Commerce was one of the busiest streets in Pine Lake, with banks, businesses, the post office, the county courthouse and the municipal police department all situated around a crowded square. The Caddo County Sheriff's Office was one street over on Center Avenue and Pine Lake High School a few blocks in the other direction on West Pleasure, an irony that had never been lost on the student body.

As Jack took in the familiar but long forgotten sights, a strange nostalgia settled over him. Before Anna's murder, he and his family had been happy in this town. His parents had been respected members of a close-knit community. His father had owned the local hardware store and his mother had worked at the First National Bank. Jack had once mowed the lawns of the same people who would later look at him with open suspicion and who had gone out of their way to cross the street when they met him on the sidewalk. Just like his onetime friends had avoided him in the school hallways and had refused to sit with him in the cafeteria.

Jack had learned the hard way that a small town could be a cruel, lonely place. By the time graduation had rolled around, Wayne Foukes was behind bars and some of Jack's classmates had begun to make overtures, but it was too late. He wanted nothing to do with any them. He hadn't even gone to his graduation ceremony, preferring instead to pack his belongings and move three hours away to an apartment near Sam Houston State University where he would pursue a major in criminal justice rather than the pre-law degree he'd once dreamed about.

None of that mattered now, of course, and Jack

berated himself for his sentimentality. He had come back to Pine Lake for one reason only—to find out why his two best friends had lied about their whereabouts on the night of Anna's murder. Emotion had no place in his investigation. He'd learned that lesson the hard way, too.

At the end of the business district, traffic thinned and the buildings grew seedier as he neared the city limits. Jack figured he'd lost the black truck for good. He started to turn around and head back toward town when he spotted the vehicle parked at the end of an alley that ran between an old tire store and an abandoned building that had once housed the Masonic Lodge. He drove on by, found a place to park and then doubled back on foot.

Two men sat on a bench in front of the tire store watching the street. They spared Jack a glance as he approached, but neither seemed to recognize him. One gave a brief nod while the other looked away quickly as if he didn't want to see too much. Jack understood. Even in a town as small as Pine Lake, there were areas where it was best to turn a blind eye.

Keeping watch on the street behind him, he walked down the alley until he could get a better view of the truck. Then he took out his phone, snapped a shot of the license plate and texted the image to one of his contacts at the Houston Police Department. He heard back in a matter of minutes: *Truck registered to Marc Waller, 212 Locust Avenue, Pine Lake, Texas.*

The name wasn't lost on Jack. The connections were becoming a little too entangled to be coinciden- tal. Strange that Tommy Driscoll hadn't recognized Waller's truck from the description. But to give him the benefit of the doubt, no county sheriff could be aware of every vehicle in his jurisdiction.

Still, Jack had to wonder why Waller had been driving so recklessly through the middle of town on the morning after his girlfriend's body had been dis- covered and even more curious, why he had seemed hell-bent on frightening Olive. Maybe anyone in that crosswalk would have had the same close call or maybe Olive was right and it was a matter of intim- idation. But Waller was no school kid and Jack was starting to have a very bad feeling. Something was going on in Pine Lake. A war, Tommy had called it. Somehow Olive was caught in the middle whether she realized it or not.

Jack put away his phone and approached the truck with caution, checking over his shoulder once again before stepping up to the side window. The cab was empty and the doors locked. His first thought was that the driver had disappeared behind the wooden fence that separated the alley from the rear of an- other dilapidated building. He opened the gate and had a quick look around, and then as he came back through, he saw that the side door of the abandoned building stood slightly ajar.

Flattening himself against the crumbling brick wall, he pushed open the door just enough to get a glimpse inside. Lit only by anemic sunbeams that filtered in through the dusty windows, the interior lay in deep shadows. He listened for a moment and then slipped inside, pausing at the threshold to take stock.

At one time, the building must have been a renovation project, but that, too, had been abandoned. He could see the skeletal outline of a two-story scaffold and the ragged curtains of poly that had sectioned off the various stages of work. Beer bottles, cigarette butts and pen casings littered the floor. An old mattress had been shoved up against one wall, a battered sofa against another. The musty scent of time and neglect hung thick in the air, along with the darker notes of urine and rodent infestation.

Unease trickled down Jack's spine. This was not a good place. The building had been derelict even when he'd lived in Pine Lake. It had always been known as a trouble spot despite its proximity to downtown. He remembered rumors of dark goings-on, everything from drug-fueled parties to satanic rituals. Once in middle school, he and Nathan and Tommy had crawled through a back window to explore, climbing to the roof from the precarious second-floor access and then descending all the way down into the basement, a cavernous place of looming shadows and glowing eyes. They'd been oblivious to the homeless man who had been living in the building until he'd rushed from a corner howling like a dog. Jack could only remember one other time when he'd been so frightened—the first day he'd been subjected to Sheriff Brannigan's vicious style of interrogation.

His senses on high alert, he moved about the dingy space, searching in corners and behind the plastic dividers. When he got to the stairs, he drew up short as his gaze traveled up the steps and through the shadows to the second-floor landing. Someone was up there. He could hear a muted voice—someone on a cell phone perhaps—but he was too far away to pick up the one-sided conversation.

Jack told himself whatever was going on inside that building was none of his business. He should leave now before he was spotted. He hadn't come to Pine Lake to involve himself in an active murder investigation and he sure as hell had no intention of breaking up a drug deal. His only interest in the driver of that black truck was the close call Olive had had with him that morning. Jack wouldn't mind having a long talk with Marc Waller about that incident.

But like it or not, Jack was involved. He'd been involved ever since he'd found Jamie Butaud's body. Maybe even earlier than that, when he'd taken that first call from Nathan Bolt. He'd been lured back to Pine Lake with the bait of the past, but the present-day circumstances had ensnared him because some of the players were the same. He didn't know if there was a connection between the two murders, but he did know that he would always be haunted by the lies surrounding Anna's death if he didn't do everything he could to put those lingering questions and suspicions to rest.

Halfway up the stairs, he froze again. The voice was getting louder, angrier. He turned an ear to the sound as he searched the shadows on the landing and then pivoted to scour the area below him. He heard nothing else. No misplaced footfalls or creaking doors, but a light breeze drifted up the stairs and feathered along his nape. Someone had come into the building and now Jack had been caught between the newcomer and the person somewhere on the second floor.

He had no choice but to abandon caution, sprint up the stairs and dart into one of the empty rooms. But as he reached the stop step, a door flew open and he found himself face to face with a man he assumed was Marc Waller. Jack assessed him in a glance. He looked just shy of six feet, thin to the point of emaciation with shoulder-length hair and a scraggly beard. More important, he was armed and Jack wasn't.

Footsteps pounded on the stairs and Jack reacted on instinct. He lunged at the man in the doorway, allowing the momentum of the impact to carry them back into the murky room. Waller's gun went flying and as he dove for the weapon, Jack tackled him. They crashed to the floor, rolling and punching and cursing hard.

As Jack straddled his opponent, he seemed to have the upper hand. He was larger and more physically fit, but Waller was a scrapper. He bucked and kicked and thrashed about until it seemed to Jack the scrawny man had superhuman strength. Still, Jack would have eventually prevailed if not for the blow to the back of his head.

Dazed, he slumped to the floor as pain exploded behind his eyeballs. He tried to clear his vision as he lashed out at his new assailant. Before he could shake off a wave of dizziness, he was pinned face-down and a moment later, he felt a prick at the base of his neck.

When he was finally released, he tried to scramble to his feet, but the room spun out of control and he discovered a sudden heaviness in his limbs. The floor pitched and he collapsed, rolling to his back to stare up at the rotating ceiling. After a moment, a strange euphoria seeped through his veins, along with a weighted lethargy. Shadows moved about the dingy room, but they didn't concern him. The voices that came to him were dreamlike and distorted. *We can't kill him. His people will come looking for him and those guys don't mess around.*

Someone knelt and peered down at him. He saw a floating star in the darkness and tried to catch it. Then he drifted away and saw nothing at all.

Chapter Six

"Jack, can you hear me? You need to wake up now. Open your eyes, please."

The brisk voice was annoyingly persuasive, but Jack didn't want to wake up. A jackhammer was going off in his head and he could taste vomit at the back of his throat. Best to just drift back into the darkness. But that voice niggled. Beneath the school-teacher calm was an edge of fear that nudged him out of his lethargy. He tunneled his way through a thick curtain of cobwebs and opened his eyes to a blurry world.

Someone hovered over him. He struggled to get up but a firm hand on his shoulder pressed him back down. "Take it easy. You'll be okay."

He groaned and put an arm over his eyes. "Where am I?"

"You're home."

"I'm in Houston?"

The voice hesitated. "No, Jack. You're in your

uncle's cabin on Pine Lake. You have a bump on the back of your head. Do you remember falling?"

He tried to swallow past all the cotton in his mouth. "No."

"What about the scrapes on your knuckles and the bruise on your cheek? Did you get into a fight?"

"Not that I recall."

Another pause. "Do you know who I am?"

"Olive Belmont."

"Yes, that's right." She sounded relieved.

He blinked to bring her into focus, vectoring in on the freckles across her nose. Her smile was soothing, but her blue eyes looked worried. He wanted to reassure her that he was fine, but the throbbing in his head wouldn't give him any peace.

He pressed fingertips into his temples. "What are you doing here?"

"Nathan called when he found you."

Jack glanced up. "Found me where?"

"Here in the cabin. He drove out to see you and noticed that the front door was open. He thought there might have been a break-in so he came inside to have a look around. He found you here on the couch. When he had trouble rousing you, he called me."

"Why you?"

She shrugged. "Nathan's always been useless in medical crises. He may be older, but I'm the one who had to deal with the blood. Not literally," she quickly added. "You're not bleeding, thank goodness."

"He was always a little squeamish," Jack agreed.

She gave a little chuckle. "See? It's all coming back. Now do you remember how you got all those bumps and bruises?"

"That's still a blank."

"Well, let's take it one step at a time. What's the last thing that you do remember?"

He answered automatically. "I saw you outside the coffee shop this morning. You had on a white dress and a black truck almost ran you down. Then you left for work and I went to see Tommy Driscoll."

"Jack." She leaned closer, staring deeply into his eyes. "What day is this?"

He frowned at the question. "It's Tuesday. I drove up from Houston late yesterday."

"It's Wednesday," she corrected. "A little after four o'clock in the afternoon. The events you cited happened yesterday morning. Are you telling me you don't remember anything since then?"

A thrill of alarm chased up his spine, along with a dark premonition that something bad had happened during his blackout. He held out his right hand, studying the raw skin on his knuckles. Now he knew how Olive felt after sleepwalking. Losing a chunk of time was terrifying.

He massaged his temples even harder, as if he could somehow resuscitate his memory. "I drove back into town for lunch. I ate at a place on Main Street and then I went by Nathan's office. As I was leaving, I saw the black truck that almost hit you. I followed it, I think."

His revelation seemed to take her aback. "Why would you do that?"

"I wanted to have a word with the driver."

"A word?" She bit her lip in consternation. "Did you?"

"I don't know."

"You don't remember a confrontation?"

"No."

"Where did you go when you followed the truck?"

"I don't know that, either."

Apprehension had slipped back into her voice. "Think about it for a minute. Do you remember a street name?"

"Commerce."

"Nathan's building is on Commerce. You already said you went by his office. Think harder. Where did you go after you left the law firm?"

"I just remember driving."

Olive looked more anxious by the moment. Jack was getting a little concerned himself. The nausea and memory loss could be symptoms of a concussion, but he didn't think so. The last twenty-four hours had been stolen by something far more insidious than a bump on his head.

She propped an arm on the back of the sofa and the other on the seat as she leaned into him, searching his face. A subtle floral fragrance emanated from her presence. Something lighter than perfume. Shampoo or a body wash, he thought. Odd that he could be so hazy about everything else and yet still be able to focus in on Olive Belmont's scent. Not to mention the vibrant blue of her eyes and the lush copper of her hair, which spilled over her shoulders and curtained her cheeks. He wanted to reach up and tangle his fingers in those thick tresses, pull her down to him for another kiss. If he closed his eyes he could still remember the taste of her on his lips—

"Jack." She touched his shoulder lightly. "You seem to be drifting. Stay with me, okay?"

"Yeah, doing my best." With an effort, he pushed himself up and swung his legs off the couch, sitting for a moment with his head in his hands as the room swam around him.

"We should get you to the emergency room. The disorientation and memory loss could be signs of concussion."

"I don't think so."

"It's best to let a doctor make that determination. Head injuries shouldn't be ignored," she insisted. "You'll need tests and several hours of monitoring. Can you walk?"

"I don't need to go to the hospital. I'll be fine."

"How can you say that when you were apparently unconscious for over twenty-four hours?"

"More like passed out."

She said in disbelief, "You were drunk?"

"Drugged would be my guess," a voice said from the entrance.

Jack lifted his head from his hands and glanced

toward the door where a man stood silhouetted on the threshold. Olive didn't seem at all surprised by her cousin's appearance, leaving Jack to conclude that Nathan Bolt had been hovering right outside the door all along.

As he came inside to join them, Jack gave the attorney a quick appraisal. Unlike Tommy Driscoll, who had softened over the years, Nathan Bolt had lost the extra weight that had stubbornly clung to him all through high school. He was trim and well-dressed with a hairstyle and round glasses that made him look both clever and earnest, especially with his loosened tie and rolled-up shirtsleeves. Jack didn't buy the Boy Scout image. He didn't trust Nathan Bolt any more than he had faith in Tommy Driscoll. Not that he cared all that much, but he couldn't help wondering what had caused their falling out. The lies they'd told after Anna's death? The natural animosity between a cop and a defense attorney? A disagreement over turf?

"Hello, Jack."

"Nathan."

"Drugged?" Olive repeated in disbelief. "Who would do such a thing?"

Nathan sat down in a chair across from the couch. He seemed perfectly at home in Leon's cabin and Jack wondered again about the discussion that had been referenced during their first phone call. Accord-

ing to Nathan, contacting Jack had been Leon's idea.
No way to prove that now, of course.

"You said you followed a black truck," Nathan
said. "My guess is, you saw something you shouldn't
have."

"Like what?" Olive demanded.

"Don't be so naïve, cousin. You know better than
anyone what's happening in this town. You see it at
school before it filters down to the rest of us."

"You think Jack stumbled onto a drug deal?"

Nathan shrugged. "Wouldn't surprise me."

"That's terrifying! But if they knocked him on
the head and drugged him, how did he get home?"

"That's a very good question." Nathan's gaze
moved from Olive to Jack. "You still look pretty out
of it so I doubt you were in any condition to drive.
Someone must have brought you here and dumped
you on the couch. Your car is in the driveway."

Jack tried to summon even a glimmer of that trip
home. Nothing. His mind was a complete blank.

"Tell me more about this black truck," Nathan
said.

"The driver almost ran Olive down this—yesterday morning."

"That's being a little dramatic," she said. "I
stepped off the curb and the truck came a little too
close for comfort. Luckily, Jack was there to pull
me back."

"That is lucky," Nathan agreed. "Are you saying
you think it was deliberate?"

"No, of course not. It was probably just a student trying to intimidate me." She glanced at Jack. "We've already been through this."

"Yes, but I'm not as convinced as you," he said.

"Nor should you be," Nathan agreed. "Marc Waller drives a black truck."

Something flashed in Jack's memory, a flickering image of a lanky man that was there one moment and gone the next. He put a hand to the back of his head, locating the knot with a wince. "New with a custom paint job?"

"*Expensive* custom paint job," Nathan said. "He came by the office a few weeks ago to show it off to Jamie. When she wouldn't leave with him, he lost his temper and created a scene. We ended up calling the police."

"What does this guy look like?" Jack asked.

"Thin, twitchy, unkempt. Has kind of a feral look in his eyes."

Olive turned to Jack with an anxious appraisal. "Do you remember seeing him?"

The image flickered again, along with a fleeting memory of muted voices, but Jack shook his head. "I can't place him. Is there any reason he'd want to hurt you?"

"Of course not," she insisted. "I barely know the man."

"Actually," Nathan said slowly, "there might be."

Olive stared at him, dumbfounded. "What do you mean?"

"You're my only family here in Pine Lake since the old man passed away. Marc knows how close we are. I wouldn't put it past him to use you to get to me."

"What? That's crazy," she said with a frown. "Why would he need to get to you, anyway? You were the one who saved him from serious jail time."

"That was a long time ago. Lately he seems to think I was trying to turn Jamie against him."

"Were you?" Jack asked.

"I helped her go back to school. I gave her a job and encouraged her to continue her education. I opened doors for her, but Marc saw it differently." Nathan paused as he eyed Olive warily. "Would you mind giving us a moment?"

Her scowl deepened. "Yes, I mind. Whatever you have to say to Jack can wait. All of this can wait. He needs to go to the emergency room."

"That's his call, not ours."

She turned back to Jack. "I'll drive you there myself. I don't mean to nag, but you really do need to see a doctor."

"I appreciate your concern," he said. "But I'm already feeling better. A couple of painkillers for the headache and I'll be my old self again."

Olive didn't look at all happy about his decision, but she shrugged in resignation. "I can't force you. I'm going back to the office for a bit and then straight home. If either of you need me, call my cell."

"Thanks for coming, cousin."

"Yes, thank you," Jack said.

She stared down at him for a moment and then with another shrug, picked up her handbag and headed for the door.

Jack had the strongest urge to call her back. She was right. Whatever Nathan Bolt had to say to him could wait. Right now, he wanted to be alone with Olive. *Needed* to be with her, but he couldn't for the life of him explain his sense of urgency.

She walked out the door and he didn't call her back. Instead, he got up and went into the kitchen on the pretext of needing water and aspirin. He stood at the sink and watched her through the window. Even for a high school principal, the navy dress and beige heels were sedate. Her appearance was understated and professional, and yet Jack felt a dangerous awareness as he took in her slight curves and the graceful sweep of red hair over one eye. She tossed the thick strands aside with a shake of her head, a movement that was unaffected and yet undeniably sensual.

As if intuiting his perusal, she turned to glance back at the house. The sunlight streaming through the window was still so bright, he didn't think she could see him, but her gaze seemed to find his through the glass. She didn't wave or nod to acknowledge his presence, but a smile flitted before she opened the door and climbed behind the wheel.

It was barely a response and yet Jack knew he would have felt the impact of that smile from a mile away.

NATHAN STOOD AT the large window that looked out on the lake. He glanced over his shoulder as Jack entered the room and then turned back to the water.

"I always did say Leon had the best view on the lake."

"Yeah, it's nice." Jack went over to the couch and plopped down on the leather cushions.

"Let me know if you decide to sell," Nathan said. "I've always wanted a place like this. A little cabin on the water where you can hunker down and get away from civilization."

"It's less than a mile from town," Jack reminded him. "But it *is* a long way from Austin."

Nathan turned with a wry smile. "So you've already tuned into the local gossip, have you?"

"I've heard some things. But you didn't drive out here to talk about politics or real estate."

Nathan shoved his hands in his pockets as he leaned a shoulder against the window frame. "No, you're right. I came to find out why you didn't let me know you were coming to Pine Lake."

"Because I didn't come here to work for you," Jack said bluntly. "I came for my own reasons. And in case you haven't heard, I've been a little busy since I got here."

"Another reason you should think about selling this place. Pine Lake seems to bring you nothing but bad luck."

Jack shrugged. "It's different this time. Unlike you, I don't have a connection to the victim."

"Oh, come on," Nathan said. "You can't think I had anything to do with Jamie's death. I never did anything but try to help that girl."

"I'm sure the sheriff will be sympathetic."

Anger flared behind the round glasses, but Nathan's expression remained composed. "Your attitude about what happened is annoyingly cavalier. Jamie's death may not mean anything to you, but a lot of people have been devastated by the news. She was a good person. Everyone in my office liked and respected her. She did her work without complaint or drama and that's a lot more than I can say for most people."

"I'm sorry for your loss," Jack said sincerely.

Nathan turned back to the water with a brooding frown. "She made mistakes when she was younger, but she learned from them. And she'd been trying ever since to turn her life around. She was even talking about going back to school to become a paralegal. But you know how it is in a place like this. The harder you work to make something of yourself, the harder others will try to tear you down."

"People like Marc Waller, you mean."

"People exactly like Marc Waller. Scum of the earth, that man."

"The one thing everyone around here seems to agree on," Jack muttered. "And yet you were not only his lawyer, you got serious charges against him dropped."

"I don't have to like my clients, but I do have to

represent them to the very best of my abilities. Even creeps like Marc Waller."

"It's a dirty job," Jack said.

"It can be." Nathan came back into the room and sat down across from Jack, leaning forward as he draped his elbows over the armrests. "Jamie had been trying to break things off for a long time, but Marc didn't take kindly to rejection. He's a violent, volatile man who seems to have little to no control over his temper. I wouldn't put anything past him if he thought she was seeing someone else."

"Even murder?"

"I think he's certainly capable."

"Was she seeing someone else?"

"I don't know. I suspected but I never saw her with anyone."

"Does Tommy know about the altercation at your office?" Jack asked.

"It's a matter of public record. Jamie filed a complaint with the Pine Lake PD. If Tommy Driscoll wants to talk to me about any of this, he knows where to find me."

"That doesn't sound very cooperative." Jack absently massaged his temples.

"Like I said, he knows where to find me." Nathan's gaze turned shrewd. "I understand you've been in to see him already."

"I'm the one who found the body and the lake area is the county sheriff's jurisdiction. I wouldn't read anything more into it than that."

"I wasn't. But I can't help wondering about suspects. He must have leads," Nathan prompted.

"I can't help you there. Tommy Driscoll isn't likely to talk to me about his investigation."

"I thought he might have let something slip."

Now it was Jack who turned sly. "Your name came up."

A shadow flickered again behind the glasses. "In what context?"

Jack waited a beat before he continued. "He told me that on the night of Anna's murder, you left the house after midnight and didn't return until nearly sunup."

"*Anna's* murder?" Nathan stared at him for a moment as he shifted gears.

"That's the bait you used to get me here. Tommy Driscoll's whereabouts on that night. Seems your movements are also in question."

Emotions flickered across Nathan's face and he grew pensive. Jack wondered if he was thinking back to that night or trying to figure out the best way to squirm out of his lie. Finally he said, "Okay. I did leave the house that night, but there was nothing sinister about my movements. I went out looking for Olive. She had a sleeping disorder back then. She would get up from her bed and wander around at all hours. It got really bad after her dad died. When she and her mother came to live with us, I developed a kind of sixth sense about her sleepwalking. Sometimes I would rouse in the middle of the night and know she was gone. When I woke up that night, Tommy was also missing. At first, I thought they might have left the house together, but Olive despised Tommy. I couldn't see her going off with him so I went out to look for her."

"Where did you find her?"

"It took me half the night, but I finally found her on Lakeside Road not far from the old bridge."

Jack's voice sharpened. "She was sleepwalking?"

"Yes."

"You didn't wake her up?"

"I never did back then. I led her back to the house and she crawled into bed as if nothing had happened."

"Let me get this straight. You're saying Olive was on or near the old bridge on the night Anna was murdered?"

Nathan's gaze burned into Jack's. "Yes. That's exactly what I'm saying. She had a perverse fascination for that bridge. She used to go there a lot. I don't know how much you remember about her circumstances, but her dad was killed in a head-on collision on a similar bridge. He'd been away on a business trip and was rushing back for Olive's birthday. It was raining, the road was slippery. His vehicle went through the guardrail after the crash. Olive blamed herself. She'd begged him to come back that night rather than wait until morning. Her mother was no help. She was so devastated she could barely look after herself let alone deal with Olive's guilt. My old man took charge and moved them in with us. Olive's mother was his baby sister. He was protective of her just the way I've always been of Olive." Nathan's gaze was still on Jack. "Do you see where I'm going with this?"

"I want to hear you say it."

"I didn't go to the police for the same reason you didn't tell Tommy the truth about Monday night." He put up a hand as if expecting Jack to interrupt. "Don't worry. Olive never said a word, but I knew she'd been sleepwalking the moment I heard what happened. She was already at the lake when you found the body, wasn't she?"

Jack said nothing.

"You made up a story because you were afraid she'd seen something. You were worried Jamie's killer would come after her if he found out she'd been there. I understand, Jack. And I can't tell you how much I appreciate your discretion."

"I didn't make up anything. Events happened just the way I reported them."

Nathan smiled. "Of course."

His smugness rankled but Jack let it go. "So you woke up that night and found both Olive and Tommy missing. How did he explain his absence?"

"He told me he'd gone out to meet someone, an older woman that he was seeing. He said there would be serious consequences if anyone ever found out about the affair. Especially for her. She might be fired or even arrested. I assumed he was seeing a teacher."

"He never mentioned a name?"

"No. It's possible he made up the story, but you remember what a horndog he was back then. Still is, from what I hear. I've never understood why Beth puts up with him."

"Maybe she loves him."

"That's even harder to understand. A guy like that? She must have known what was going on behind her back. All those girls in school coming on to him, following him around like a bunch of damn groupies. It was disgusting." Nathan's expression hardened. "You know what he told me once? He said he'd actually talked some of those girls into getting the same tattoo. His mark, he called it. He laughed at their gullibility. He didn't care about their feelings. It was just a game to him. Like cutting notches in a bedpost."

"We all did stupid things back then," Jack said. "I never heard about the tattoos."

"Of course not. Tommy liked to brag to me, but he looked up to you. He always wanted your approval."

"I don't know about that."

"I know," Nathan said. "I saw a side of Tommy Driscoll you never did. He wasn't just mean, he could be downright vicious. A bully in every sense of the word. You asked earlier if I thought Marc Waller killed Jamie. I don't discount the possibility, but he's not the only one with a motive. A few months after

Jamie came to work for me, the air conditioner in the office went out. It was sweltering inside the building so I sent everyone home. Jamie volunteered to stay and answer the phones. She always wore long sleeves in the office to cover her tattoos, but that day she'd taken off her sweater. I saw Tommy's tattoo—his *mark*—on her shoulder."

"You think she was seeing him?"

"I doubt that tattoo was a coincidence. Think about it, Jack. Tommy Driscoll is a married man. That alone gives him a motive, but Jamie was still underage when she first came to work for me. If she and Tommy were seeing each other that far back and if she threatened to expose the affair now, what do you think he'd do? Jack? Are you listening to me?"

Nathan's voice receded to a dull roar. The sudden churning in Jack's stomach had nothing to do with the drug he'd been given. A memory had surfaced, distant and hazy at first, but now the image sharpened as if he'd adjusted a focus ring. He got up and paced to the window, staring down at the water with a brooding frown as his mind tumbled back to a mild fall night on Anna's front porch.

She and some of her girlfriends had gone to Dallas for the weekend. She'd come back with a tattoo of a heart shot through with a lightning bolt, laughing sheepishly when Jack had first discovered it on her hip.

I had a little too much to drink...someone dared me... Do you hate it?

No, I like it. It's sexy. But I'm trying to figure out what the lightning bolt means.

It doesn't mean anything. It was just a whim. A stupid mistake.

Maybe if I could have a closer look...

Stop! My dad could come out here any second. Do you know what he'd do if he found us like this?

I thought you liked to live dangerously.

Maybe I do. Jack?

Hmm?

I love you. You know that, right? You're the best thing that's ever happened to me, but sometimes I wonder...what if I'm not the girl you think I am? Jack? Are you even listening to me?

"Jack?"

He turned. "What did the tattoo look like? The one on Jamie Butaud's shoulder?"

Nathan gave a contemptuous snort. "It was a heart with a lightning bolt rammed through the center. Real subtle. Just like Tommy Driscoll."

Chapter Seven .

After a shower and several glasses of cold water, Jack started to feel human again. He grabbed a beer and headed down to the dock to enjoy the last of the sunset. The past twenty-four hours remained a mystery, but the harder he tried to recover those lost memories, the more painful the throbbing in his head became. He told himself to relax. Bit and pieces would come back in due time.

But he still had a nagging worry that something bad had happened during his blackout. Had he found the driver of the black truck? Had he confronted Marc Waller face to face? Had they fought? Jack had no recollection of a conversation, let alone an altercation, but something needled at the back of his mind as he massaged his banged-up knuckles.

Halfway down the steps, he came to an abrupt halt. A woman sat on the edge of the dock, dangling her feet in the water. His first thought was that Olive had come back, but as he descended a few more stairs, he saw that the woman's hair was dark and clipped short.

"Can I help you?" he called out.

She started at the sound of his voice and scrambled to her feet, turning with a wry smile as her gaze traveled up the steps to where he waited. "Hello, stranger!" she called back.

He stared down at her for a moment. "Beth? Beth Driscoll?"

She laughed. "Oh, good! You remember me!"

"Of course, I remember you." He descended the rest of the steps to join her.

Dressed in a simple cotton skirt and sleeveless blouse, she looked young and carefree standing in the afterglow of the sunset—just the way Jack remembered her. Even the short hair was the same. But as he drew closer, he couldn't help noticing the lines around her eyes and at the corners of her mouth. The hardness in her stare and the brittle quality of her smile. His old friend was far from carefree. Marriage to Tommy Driscoll had been no picnic.

"I heard you were back," she said.

"Word always did travel fast around here."

She motioned to the edge of the dock where her sandals had been abandoned. "I hope you don't mind my dropping by like this. It's still so hot out and the water looked inviting. I couldn't resist."

"I don't mind, but you could have just knocked on my door."

A cloud flitted across her expression. "I meant to, but somehow I lost my nerve when I got out here."

"Why would it take nerve to knock on my door? I don't bite," he said as they stood awkwardly facing one another.

Her laugh was self-conscious. "I know that. It's just…" She trailed off. "This is crazy." She closed the distance between them and gave him a quick hug.

He returned the embrace, taking note of her slenderness. She wasn't naturally slight like Olive, and Jack wondered about the weight loss that had stripped away her curves and revealed too much of her collarbone. Her arms and legs looked as fragile and hollow as bird bones.

She said against his shoulder, "It shouldn't be this hard to greet an old friend."

"I wasn't sure I had any friends left in this town."

She pulled away, searching his face. "I know it must have seemed that way back then, but I never stopped being your friend." Her hand came up to flutter against his bruised cheek. "You were always good to me, Jack."

He frowned. "Was I?"

"You don't remember?"

He shrugged as he set the beer on the railing. "I don't dwell too much on those days."

She turned to stare out over the water. "I've always regretted not standing by you when things got so bad. It was never about guilt or innocence. I let you down because I was too wrapped up in my own

problems. That's no excuse. And none of this probably means anything to you now. But..." She trailed
off on another nervous laugh. "I'm not very good
at this."

"You're fine."

"I just need you to know that I always believed
in you. That's why I'm here. That's why I came.
And ultimately, that's why I couldn't bring myself
to knock on your door. Because I'm about fifteen
years too late."

"Why now?" he asked without rancor.

"Because you're back and because I've always
wanted to say these things to you. The way you were
treated. It was disgraceful. *We* were disgraceful." She
tilted her head to stare deeply into his eyes. "You
were the best part of this town. Nothing has ever
been the same since you left."

"I somehow doubt that." Her words touched a
nerve. Whether good or bad, Jack wasn't sure.

"It's true." She walked over to the edge of the
dock, peering as intently into the water as she had
into his eyes. "This place brings back a lot of memories," she said on a shiver. "Remember how we used
to come out here at night and swim in the moonlight?
You and me and Tommy and Anna. They were such
vibrant creatures, weren't they? So full of life. I was
a wallflower and you were always so intense. I used
to secretly wonder if we'd made the wrong choice.
The wrong pairing. Maybe you and I would have
been better suited."

"I don't know how well suited I am to anyone," Jack said in a moment of candor. "But you and Tommy have been together for a long time. You seemed to have made a go of it."

"You've been away from Pine Lake for too long. Things around here are rarely as they seem."

Jack thought of that tattoo on Jamie Butaud's shoulder and the one on Anna's hip. A heart with a lightning bolt shot through the center. Tommy Driscoll's mark. A symbol that connected two murders fifteen years apart.

Beth was staring at him over her shoulder, a smile flitting at the corners of her mouth. He had never known her to be coy or sly and yet there was something about that smile that sent a warning up his spine.

You asked if I thought Marc Waller killed Jamie. He's certainly capable. But he isn't the only one with a motive.

"What problems?" he asked abruptly.

"I'm sorry?"

"You said you were caught up in your own problems back then. What was going on in your life?"

The question seemed to catch her off guard. "Oh, you know. The usual stuff. Everything seems a matter of life and death at that age."

Jack wondered about her sudden reticence. He walked over to the edge of the dock, staring into the murky depths just as she'd done. Something plopped in the water and the ripples distorted her reflection.

Jack watched, fascinated. Beth Driscoll seemed ephemeral in that moment. Not altogether real. It occurred to him that she had always been like that. Elusive and transitory with no lasting impression.

He saw her shiver as if she were thinking strange thoughts, too.

"Do you remember that trip you and Anna took to Dallas the fall of our senior year? A whole group of you went. She said things got a little crazy."

Beth turned with a wide-eyed stare. "That's what she told you about that trip? Things got a little crazy?"

"Didn't they?"

"That trip was a lot of things, but I would never describe it as crazy. Not the way you seem to mean it."

"How would you describe it?"

She seemed momentarily distracted as she leaned over the water to gaze past him. "I didn't know you could see the bridge from here," she murmured.

"You never could before. I think some trees have gone down. Lightning strikes, most likely." He waited a beat. "Tell me about that trip, Beth."

She sighed as her focus returned to the water. "I haven't let myself think about it for a very long time."

"What happened?"

"We didn't go to Dallas to party. At least, Anna and I didn't. That whole girls' weekend was just a cover. She and I went to an abortion clinic."

The shock was like a physical blow, punching the air from his lungs in a painful rush. "She was pregnant?"

Beth put a soothing hand on his arm. "No, not Anna. We went there for me."

Emotions swept through him. Fifteen years had dulled the pain of Anna's death, but coming back here…finding out all these things about her and the people who had once been his friends had ripped open old wounds. How had he ever thought he could remain aloof from those memories? He hadn't left Pine Lake behind. This town and these people would always be a part of him, of the boy he'd been and the man he'd become. Protective walls could only keep out so much.

The dock swayed beneath his feet and he struggled to regain his footing.

"I'm sorry," Beth said. "You look so distressed. I shouldn't have blurted it out that way. You were bound to think it was Anna."

"Did Tommy know?"

"You're assuming the baby was his."

"I'm sorry. I did assume."

She smiled. "I didn't tell him because I didn't go through with it. I decided to keep the baby no matter what he or anyone else said. Anna brought me home and I holed up in my room for the rest of the weekend. We'd already told everyone we were in Dallas and I didn't want to answer a bunch of questions about why I'd come back early. It was easier to hide out, and I needed time to think anyway."

"What about Anna?"

She shrugged. "I always assumed she drove back to Dallas to be with the others."

But maybe she hadn't rejoined the others that weekend. Maybe she'd been off somewhere getting Tommy Driscoll's mark tattooed on her hip.

Now it was Jack who drew a deep breath as he tried to sort through his feelings. The betrayal didn't matter. Not after all this time. He was too old to harbor grudges or carry torches, but he did care about the consequences. He did care about all the lies. Someone had killed Anna in cold blood. For the longest time, her murder had been considered a motiveless crime that had happened because of a chance encounter with a monster. Jack had never bought into the premise. It had always seemed personal to him, but he'd never had any legitimate suspects. He'd never been able to connect any of those troublesome dots. After a while, it became easier to just let it go. Then two old friends had called out of the blue last Friday night and here he was, back in Pine Lake chasing his past.

"What happened to the baby?" he asked. "If it's not too painful to talk about."

"I had a miscarriage. The stress of the pregnancy and then Anna's death…it was all too much, I guess."

"I'm sorry."

"It was a long time ago. Like you, I don't dwell on

it the way I used to. Life goes on." She paused, running fingers through her short tresses. "It's funny. Anna was the only other person who knew about my pregnancy and now here I am telling you about the miscarriage. I don't know why except…" Another pause. "You were always easy to talk to. I could tell you things I could never tell Tommy."

"I don't remember you ever confiding in me before."

"Don't you?" Her smile seemed wistful. "Maybe I told you more than you realized."

"I'm sorry if that's true."

"It doesn't matter anymore. I just wanted you to know why I wasn't around when you were going through all that trouble. It was a dark time and I was pretty far gone myself that year."

"Understandable."

"And now you're back," she said on another sigh.

The sun had dipped below the horizon and already Jack could sense twilight creeping in from the pine forest. The bullfrogs sang with the crickets as nostalgia settled over the landscape. When he was younger, his uncle used to say that the lake had two personalities—one by day and one by night. He wondered about the woman who stood beside him. He could no longer see her reflection in the water, but when he glanced at her profile, she seemed stoic and unassuming. Did more secrets lurk beneath that calm surface?

"I should go," she said as if sensing his scrutiny. "I'm glad you've finally come home. It's been too long."

Would she welcome him back when she learned of his agenda?

"I need to ask you something before you go," he said.

He could sense a sudden tension that made him wonder.

"What is it?"

"How well did you really know Anna?"

A shadow fell across her expression. "That's an odd question. I knew her for most of my life. So did you. We all went to kindergarten together."

"You said she was the only person you told about the pregnancy. Did she confide in you?"

"Of course. That's what girlfriends do."

"Did you know she was seeing someone else?"

The shadow fleeted again. "I don't believe that. Not for a second. Anna would never have cheated on you. She loved you."

"Did she?"

"Yes, of course, she did." Her voice turned ironic. "Besides, it's hard to hide infidelity in a town this small."

"Maybe this town has more secrets than you know." He was still gazing down at her. Her eyes seemed guileless, but who really knew? "That night has always haunted me. I dropped Anna off early. She waited until I was gone and then she slipped back out of her house. It's logical to assume she went out to meet someone."

"Maybe she just went for a walk."

"Alone? At that time of night?"

"It wasn't that late. Anna was a night owl, remember?"

"You didn't talk to her that night? You don't have any idea who she may have gone out to meet?"

"Jack." She placed her hand on his arm. He wondered if she used the same appeasing gesture to calm Tommy's temper. "Why are you letting this get to you now? We've all moved on."

"Have we? Then why did you come out here to talk to me?"

"I told you why. I wanted to apologize, not dredge up all that old pain. Why torment yourself with all those unanswered questions?"

"I'm just looking for the truth, Beth."

She was silent for a moment. "You never believed Wayne Foukes killed her, did you?"

"No."

"Yet you never tried to free him. You never spoke out against his incarceration."

"You don't know what I did," Jack said. "Just because I didn't shout about it from the middle of Main Street doesn't mean I kept those doubts to myself. But the law doesn't put a lot of stock in gut feelings. Especially coming from someone like me."

"Is that why you've come back now?" she asked. "Because of a gut feeling?"

"It's a little more substantial than that."

She frowned. "I don't understand. You have new evidence?"

"Let's just say, I've heard differing accounts of what happened that night. At the very least, lies were told to the police. I intend to find out why."

"No matter who you hurt?"

"What are you afraid of?"

"You misunderstand me." She took a step toward him, so quickly he didn't have time to move away. Her hand fluttered again to his bruised cheek. "I'm not afraid, Jack. I've been waiting fifteen years for the truth to come out."

OLIVE STOOD AT the top of the wooden steps gazing down at the couple on the dock. Jack and Beth Driscoll were old friends and so it came as no surprise to see them together. Yet for some strange reason, Olive felt blindsided. Not because she was jealous or envious or even all that curious about their conversation, but because observing Jack in such an unguarded moment took her breath away.

A panicky tremor shot through her and she could feel a warning prickle all across her scalp. Her intense awareness of him shocked and frightened her, which was crazy. What was there to fear? She was a grown woman and she'd hardly lived her life as a hermit. She'd even been in love once or twice. But the amiable farewells when the relationships ended had only reinforced the necessity of those partings.

Breakups shouldn't be so easy. Not if there'd been real passion. Estrangements should be agonizingly tearful with unwise recriminations and long, sleepless nights. Olive had walked away with only a mild sense of regret. Her partners had seemed to feel the same. One had married within six months of their separation, the other had moved out of state. Olive wished them well but not enough to keep up with their lives. If she never saw either of them again, it would be no great loss.

But Jack…

Her trepidation deepened as she watched him in the waning light. Already she dreaded the time when he would pack his bags and leave town, most likely for good this time. In many ways, Olive was still the hopeless romantic she'd been at fourteen and a part of her was irresistibly drawn to the notion of the prodigal son. But this was more than a fantasy or a lingering schoolgirl crush. Somehow in the space of forty-eight hours, she'd developed real feelings for Jack King.

This would not end well, she predicted as she smoothed clammy hands down the sides of her jeans. He'd come to Pine Lake to settle old scores. Getting between a man and his mission was never a good idea. Beth Driscoll would do well to remember that, too.

Olive started toward the dock, letting her sneakers thump against the wooden stairs to alert them of her presence. When Jack turned, she waved and called out a greeting.

"Sorry! I didn't mean to interrupt," she said as she stepped onto the dock. The gentle sway of the platform made her feel light-headed. She put a hand on the rail to steady herself.

"I was just leaving." Beth bent to retrieve her sandals, hooking the heel straps over her index finger. As she straightened, her gaze settled on Olive. "We haven't had a chance to talk all summer, but I've been meaning to call and congratulate you on the promotion. I'm looking forward to the new school year."

Olive studied her in the dusky light. She looked sincere but there was an indefinable edge in her voice. "Thanks, Beth. I'm looking forward to the year, as well."

"I have some suggestions for the science lab. Maybe we can schedule a time to talk in the next week or so."

"Yes, of course. I'll be in my office every day until at least five."

"I'll be sure and stop by." Beth turned back to Jack. "It was really good to see you again. Don't be such a stranger from now on."

"I'll be around for a few days," he said. "Maybe we'll see each other again."

"I hope so. Goodbye for now."

"Goodbye."

Olive glanced up at Jack. His expression was in-scrutable as he watched Beth climb the steps. Once she'd disappeared into the shadows, he seemed to shrug off his contemplative mood.

"Sorry again for the interruption," she said.

"You didn't interrupt anything."

"Still, I should have called instead of dropping by this way. I've been worried about that bump on your head. I wanted to make sure you're okay and I didn't trust you to tell me the truth on the phone."

"I feel fine. Headache's almost gone. No dizziness or disorientation."

"How's the memory?"

"Still hazy but I'm hoping it'll come back."

She nodded to the sweating bottle he'd set on the dock rail. "Are you going to drink that?"

"It's probably warm by now. I can go up to the house and get you a cold one," he offered.

"Only if you're having one, too."

He hesitated. "Maybe it's best if I stick to water for now."

"Then I'll take that one off your hands." He gave her the bottle and she took a thirsty drink. "Sorry. I needed that. It's been a long day."

"You don't have to keep apologizing."

"I feel like I do. I keep barging into your life. But I guess I'm not the only one. Word has gotten around about your return and now all your old friends want to see you."

"They want something," he muttered.

"What's that supposed to mean?"

"Don't mind me. I'm being cynical."

"You're entitled. I sensed some antagonism between you and Nathan earlier." When he didn't respond, she plunged on. "I love my cousin, but I'm enough of a realist to know that he usually has an angle for everything he does. Beth, though. She seems like a straight arrow. Were you close in school?"

"I don't know about close. We were friends."

"I can still remember all of you together," Olive said dreamily. "You and Anna and Beth and Tommy. I thought of you as the beautiful people. You were like movie stars to me. Poor Nathan was always the odd man out."

"He didn't seem to mind."

"Of course, he minded. He just never let on." She leaned her forearms against the rail, still cradling the bottle. "He always gave the impression of having it all together, but he was a mess in high school. He just never let anyone see it. I'm sure he still has his moments, but God forbid he should ever let down his guard."

"What do you mean by mess?"

"Don't you remember how competitive he was? How he constantly needed to prove himself?" Olive felt a little disloyal to her cousin for speaking so forthrightly behind his back. "His father was very domineering. He was good to my mother and me and I'll never forget the way he took us in when we were both falling apart. But he was always on Nathan's back, always finding fault, always berating him for some perceived shortcoming. I don't know how Nathan turned out as well-adjusted as he has."

Jack turned to stare at her. "You think he's well-adjusted?"

She laughed. "Relatively speaking. We all have our weaknesses. Mine is sleepwalking and a pathological fear of falling."

"If those are the worst of your weaknesses, I'd say you're in pretty good shape."

"Maybe so." The intensity of his look tingled all along her backbone. She focused on the water to mask her disquiet. "It's nice out here," she said after a moment. "I've always loved this lake. It's so eerie and primal. Listen." She cocked her head. "That was an alligator bellowing."

"The eggs have hatched," Jack said. "And the mothers are protective of their babies. Not a good time to go swimming."

"I'll keep that in mind. Personally, if I owned this place, I would just sit here on the dock all day and night and watch the wildlife. From a safe distance, of course."

"Maybe you'll get your chance," Jack said. "Nathan wants to buy the cabin."

Olive turned in alarm. "You're not going to sell, are you? It's your decision, of course, but I hope you don't. Leon loved this place. He'd be so happy knowing you're here even if you only manage a weekend now and then."

"We'll see," Jack said noncommittally. He motioned to the deck chairs. "Can you stay?"

"For a bit." Olive had nothing on her agenda until the following morning, but she didn't want Jack to think she was settling in for the night.

They sat side by side on the dock, cooled by a soft breeze that blew through the pine trees. The lake grew still and shadowy, a haunted forest of drowned trees and trailing moss. Sinewy bodies glided through the dark shallows. Frogs plopped, herons fished and the water lilies closed up tight, their bloom heads drooping drowsily in the waning light.

Darkness fell swiftly, a moment of complete blackness before the moon rose over the treetops. Olive placed the beer bottle on the dock between the chairs and then tipped her head back to stare up at the sky. Her nerve endings were taut and strumming. Jack was right there beside her, so near she could reach out and stroke a fingertip along his arm. All she had to do was turn her head, part her lips in invitation and she knew that he would kiss her. She wanted him to kiss her. More than anything at that moment. But she kept her gaze focused on the night sky because the last thing she needed was to get in over her head.

Beside her, Jack stirred. She could feel his gaze on her, but she didn't turn. Instead she said softly, "It really is an extraordinary place."

"I'd forgotten what it's like out here. Nothing but moonlight and water and the sound of all that nightlife."

"Not the kind of nightlife you're accustomed to," she teased.

"No."

"Do you like living in the city?"

"I like the anonymity."

She said in surprise, "But you have friends in Houston, don't you? Coworkers, acquaintances. People know who you are."

"They know my name. They know what I do for a living. They don't know me."

Olive swallowed, daring to probe deeper. "There's no one special?"

"No, not anymore."

She waited, wondering if he would elaborate.

"I was married for a time," he said with reluctance. "It didn't take."

"What happened?"

"We decided we were better friends than spouses. We ended things on good terms."

Olive liked the idea of Jack being on good terms with his ex. No tears, no recriminations, no sleepless nights. No unrequited love. No pent-up passion. "I've never married," she said. "I came close a couple of times but they didn't take, either."

He picked up the beer from the dock and lifted

the bottle to his lips. The gesture seemed unbearably intimate in the dark.

Olive shivered and searched for a safe topic. "Earlier when Nathan asked for a word alone with you, what did he want? You don't have to tell me, of course. But I can't help thinking it had something to do with me."

"He knows you were sleepwalking Monday night."

"You told him?"

"He guessed. For the record, I didn't confirm. I think it's best we stick to our story even with Nathan."

She glanced at him with a frown. "You don't think he had anything to do with Jamie's death, do you? He was very fond of her. He did a lot to help her."

Jack's gaze met hers in the moonlight. "Did you know that he lied about his whereabouts on the night Anna was murdered?"

"What?"

"He and Tommy swore they were home all night, which gave each of them an alibi. But they lied. Both of them left the house at some point."

"Surely you don't think—" She placed her hand on his arm and then she didn't quite know what to do, jerk it away or leave it there. She slid it back to the arm of her chair. "What motive would either have for killing Anna?"

"I never said they killed her. But they lied and I'd like to know why."

"Did you ask Nathan?"

"He told me that he'd gone out to find you. He said you were sleepwalking that night."

The evening was balmy, but an icy breath blew down her collar. *Had* she gone out that night? She remembered sleeping in the next morning. The sun had been warm and bright in her room when her mother had awakened her to tell her the news. Like everyone else, Olive had been devastated by the tragedy. Anna Grayson's brutal murder had rocked the whole town. To think that Olive may have been out wandering around in the dark when it happened—

"You don't remember?" Jack prodded.

"No. But I rarely recalled anything that happened during an episode. I told you before, amnesia is common in sleepwalking." She'd been gripping the chair arms, but now she made an effort to relax. "Did Nathan say where he found me?"

"On Lakeside Road near the bridge."

"The bridge…" Olive's heart thudded painfully as she stared at Jack in horror. "That's a disturbing coincidence."

"You never knew about any of this?"

She tried to shake off the glacial fingers that gripped her spine. "Nathan never said a word. You… don't think I had anything to do with Anna's death, do you? Or Jamie's?"

"Of course not."

"But you think I saw something."

"It's possible."

"I didn't," she said almost desperately. "My mind is a complete blank. Just like yours is for the past twenty-four hours. I even asked Mona Sutton about the possibility of recovering memories through hypnosis. She said the procedure would be unreliable at best."

"I imagine that's true. But if you ever want to give it a try, I know someone in Houston who could help you."

Someone he'd worked with? Someone he'd seen professionally? "I'll keep that in mind. Jack?"

"Yes?"

She'd meant to ask him something else regarding Nathan's visit, but instead she sat forward in her chair suddenly, her gaze traveling along the moonlit channel. "There's a light down there. Look. I think someone is on the bridge."

Chapter Eight

Jack swung around, searching the darkness and then rising quickly to stride to the edge of the dock. He stood for a moment tracking the light before he turned back to her. "Wait here. I'm going down there to have a look."

"In the boat?" Of course, in the boat. Did she think he was going to swim to the bridge?

He was already loosening the dock lines. She got up to help. "Let me go with you."

"It's best if you stay here."

"Why? What do you expect to find?"

He glanced back toward the flickering light. "Someone's walking the bridge with a flashlight. The better question is, what do they hope to find?"

"Evidence," she said on a surge of excitement. "Something that got left behind."

"Possibly."

"Even more reason I should go with you. Another pair of eyes." Or another target. She wasn't a particularly brave person. Where was all this sudden pluckiness coming from?

Jack stepped down in the boat and reluctantly offered her a hand. "We'll leave the lights off. He'll hear the outboard, but he may not be able to place the sound until we're already closing in."

Olive was buzzing from head to toe. "Sounds like a plan."

He gave her a warning look. "Running dark is risky in this water. If we hit a stump, we may have to swim ashore."

"Duly noted." She jumped down into the boat and then Jack started the outboard, slowly backing out into the channel. Once he'd cleared the dock, he turned the wheel sharply and hit the throttle. The boat swung around so swiftly, Olive almost lost her balance. She sat down hard and clutched the edge of the seat as the bow lifted out of the water. Jack hit the trim button and they picked up speed, skimming across the dark surface as if the devil himself were behind them. Olive liked the lake and she liked boats, but racing through a dark, perilous channel, possibly toward a murderer, was a thrill like nothing she'd ever experienced.

Behind the wheel, Jack was little more than a silhouette. She watched his profile for a moment and then turned to peer through the flying darkness as the wind buffeted her face and tore at her hair.

He didn't back off the throttle until they approached the bridge and then he shifted into idle speed. The flashlight Olive had spotted earlier was nowhere to be seen. Undoubtedly, the searcher had taken to the woods as soon as he'd heard the outboard. But as Olive scoured the shadowy deck, she could have sworn she saw a dark figure huddled near the guardrail.

"There!" she shouted over the rumble of the motor.

Jack flipped on the spotlight and the powerful beam tunneled through the darkness, leaping out of the water to climb the iron support beams. Olive almost expected to see glowing eyes in a pale face staring back at them. There was nothing but shadows.

Jack turned off the engine and they sat in inky silence as he played the light all along the bridge and up into the truss. Olive traced the beam, shivering as she imagined herself up there asleep but a part of her brain still cognizant.

A car engine sounded in the distance. Jack started the outboard and plowed toward the bank, heedless of the choking green coils clutching at the propeller. As they entered shallow water, he put the throttle in neutral, hopped out and then turned to push the hull back toward the open water. "Can you handle the wheel?"

"Yes, but what about you?"

He was already gone, wading ashore and then running through the woods toward the road. Olive took the wheel, slowly reversing away from the bank and trying her best to avoid those perilous tentacles.

Once in deeper water, she turned the boat and headed into the channel, but she felt like a sitting duck in the moonlight. She glided up under the bridge and found a place to tie off.

She sat in the rocking boat and listened to the night. The car engine had long since receded and she heard nothing from Jack. The air was very still. She seemed completely alone on the water and yet she had the strangest feeling that she was being watched. She grew uneasy and fearful. Perhaps hiding out underneath the bridge wasn't such a good idea.

She thought about starting the trolling motor and making a pass along the bank to see if she could find Jack. Surely he would have called out to her if he'd returned, but an awfully long time had passed. What if he'd run into trouble? What if he had caught and confronted Jamie Butaud's murderer? Or worse, been ambushed?

On and on Olive's thoughts churned as she huddled in the boat and waited. After a bit, the feeling came to her again that she was being watched. She scanned the banks and treetops and just as she was about to start the motor and head back into the passage, footsteps sounded overhead. Someone was on the bridge.

She wanted to believe Jack had come back and she had the strongest urge to call out to him. Whoever had been up there earlier with a flashlight would have fled once he or she heard the sound of an approaching boat. That person was probably already in town by now. But what if he wasn't? What if he'd driven down the road, parked and doubled back in order to continue his search?

What if that person had seen Jack disembark and head into the woods, leaving Olive alone on the lake?

What if he knew that she'd been on the bridge the night Jamie Butaud's body had been thrown into the water and had come back to eliminate the only witness?

Olive's imagination exploded as her heart thundered. She kept her gaze trained on the underside of the deck, following the footfalls, and didn't notice that the boat had drifted too close to the support. The scraping sound jolted her. She pushed off and tried to use the paddle to keep free of the pier, but the water lapping against the fiberglass hull sounded as loud as a crashing wave.

A light shone through the floorboards and then almost immediately went out. Olive pictured someone on the deck staring down into the water. At her. She told herself she was hidden in the shadows. No way could she be spotted. But for all she knew, she had been stalked from the moment she'd backed away from the bank.

She felt for the spotlight and then angled the bulb upward. If she flipped the switch, she might be able to catch a glimpse of whoever was up there through the cracks in the floorboards. She gathered her nerve to do exactly that when another sound came to her.

A metallic click that might have been the chamber-check of a weapon.

Olive reacted instinctively, casting off as she started the outboard. She pushed away from the support and pressed the throttle forward as she cleared the bridge.

A bullet hit the water in front of her, another beside her. She hunkered behind the wheel until she was out of range and then she brought the boat around to neutral. Water sloshed against the hull, pushing her toward the bank, but she couldn't worry about aquatic entanglements. Someone had just shot at her. Twice.

If not for a powerful surge of adrenaline, she might have collapsed from shock. Instead, she angled the spotlight toward the bridge, playing the beam all along the guardrail and into the shadows on the far side of the deck. No one was there.

For a moment, Olive wondered if she had imagined the footsteps, if she had fantasized the pepper of bullets in the water. Then she saw another form sprinting across the bridge, unmindful of the rotting floorboards and creaking support beams. She was too far away to see his features, but she knew that it was Jack. He had seen something, too. Or else the sound of gunfire had brought him running. Olive kept her gaze on that racing silhouette as she goosed the throttle and the boat shot forward.

He was gone by the time she got back to the bridge. She cruised through the first span, turned and coasted back through the other. After a couple of passes, she heard Jack calling to her from the deck. She eased into the channel until she could see him. He walked back and forth along the guardrail, the beam from his flashlight app trained on the floorboards.

"Pick me up over there," he called down to her. He motioned to the opposite bank where he'd disembarked earlier.

She found an opening in the vegetation and glided through until the bow ran aground. Jack pushed off and climbed aboard.

"Are you okay?" he asked anxiously.

"I'm fine." She took a moment to catch her breath. "Jack, someone shot at me just now. He was on the bridge."

"I heard." Anger edged his voice as his hand came up to tuck back the hair that had blown loose from her ponytail. "Are you sure you're okay."

"I think so." As adrenaline subsided, shock pummeled her. She lifted a trembling hand, observing it almost dispassionately in the moonlight. "Maybe you should take the wheel."

"Okay. But something tells me you could get us out of here just fine," he said as he slid into the bucket seat.

A FEW MINUTES LATER, they floated up to the dock and Jack tied off at the cleats. They climbed the steps in silence and once they were inside the cabin, he went straight to the kitchen and poured them both a healthy shot of whiskey.

"Better not," she said when he handed her the glass. "I still have to drive home."

"Suit yourself." He set the glass on the counter nearby. "But there's no need to drive home. You can stay here tonight. In fact, I think it would be a good idea if you did." Before she could accept or protest, he nodded toward the living room. "I'll take the couch and you can have the bed."

"That's… I appreciate the offer, but I really should go home. I have an early day tomorrow and…" She trailed away, realizing how silly it sounded to worry over mundane things like meetings and budgets when she could have been killed moments earlier. "On second thought…" She picked up the glass and downed the contents in one swallow, gasping out loud at the burn in her throat. "That's potent."

"Leon liked the good stuff." Jack carried his glass with him as he checked the front entrance and then the door to the deck. "Has your alarm been installed yet?"

"They're coming tomorrow," Olive said. "Another reason I should get home."

"Not a good idea to be there alone, at least until your security system is activated."

She turned on the barstool to watch him make his rounds. "You think whoever shot at me from the bridge would come to my house?"

"What makes you think he wouldn't?"

"What makes either of us assume the shooter was male? I never got a good look."

Jack shrugged. "Law of averages. Gut instinct. A professional guess. The point is, you need to be careful until we figure this thing out."

He made it sound as if they were in this together. Partners in crime, so to speak.

Olive didn't mind that notion at all. "Shouldn't we call the police?"

"That's not a good idea." He gave her a grim look. "I don't trust Tommy Driscoll."

"What about the Pine Lake Police Department?"

"This area is out of their jurisdiction. They'd just refer the call to the County Sheriff's Office."

"Jack?"

"Yes?"

"Is there anyone in this town you do trust?"

"No," he answered frankly. "Although after seeing the way you handled that boat just now, I can think of few people I'd rather have at my back."

"My father and I used to do a lot of fishing and skiing. He made sure I knew how to drive in case anything happened to him. And for the record, you can trust me."

"For the record, I don't *not* trust you. But Nathan Bolt is your cousin and I don't at all trust him."

"Fair enough." Olive followed him into the living room and sat down heavily on the sofa. Folding her arms around her middle, she watched as he restlessly prowled the cabin. "You're nervous," she said.

"Wired. Adrenaline always makes me jittery."

"Who do you think was on the bridge tonight?"

"I can't answer that. Like you, I never got close enough to catch a glimpse. But whatever he—or she—was looking for was important enough to risk detection. He must have taken to the woods as soon as he heard the outboard. Maybe the suspect drove away or maybe his car was just that well hidden. I never saw it. At any rate, the person doubled back to the bridge, maybe to continue the search or maybe because he knew you would be there alone."

"That's a whole lot of maybes," she said.

"Best I can do right now."

"I was under the bridge when he came back. He stood right over me. I heard footsteps. I even heard the click of a weapon. He shot in the water as I headed out to the channel, but he never came close to hitting me. Maybe his intention was to scare me."

"Another maybe."

"Best I can do," she said with a tremulous smile. "All these close calls are curious, though. You would think if someone wanted to hurt me, they could have done so by now. Maybe it really is as simple as Marc Waller wanting to get to Nathan through me."

"Nothing about this is simple," Jack said. "I do know that at first light, we need to get down there and search that bridge."

We again.

"As much as I appreciate you looking out for me, I can't stay here tonight. I don't even have a toothbrush." Her feeble attempt to lighten the mood fell flat as she searched for a more substantial excuse.

Jack's dark gaze took her in. "Lucky for you, my uncle kept plenty of spares."

"That is lucky. Jack?"

"Yes?"

"Do you have a weapon?"

"I do."

"Here in the cabin?"

"Yes."

"Why don't you carry it?"

He paused. "I'm not a big fan of guns. I carry on a need-to basis."

She glanced at him in surprise. "But you were a cop." When he merely shrugged, she said, "Why did you leave the police department?"

"I figured out I was better suited to private security. My superiors would tell you that I didn't play well with others."

"Why do I get the feeling there's more to the story?" she murmured.

"There's always more to every story." He brought the bottle in from the kitchen to replenish their glasses.

"I thought you were going to stick to water," she reminded him.

"Tomorrow I go back to water."

He poured her another drink. She took a sip and set the glass on the coffee table. "What do we do now?"

"I could fix some dinner. Are you hungry?"

"I'm still too shaky to eat."

"If you're going to keep drinking that whiskey, you need something in your stomach," he said. "Just sit there and relax. I'll see what I can rustle up."

"Jack?"

"Yes?"

"Who do you think killed Anna?"

His eyes took on a faraway look as he scrubbed the back of his hand along the scruff on his lower jaw. He appeared as rugged and capable as ever, but somehow vulnerable. Not fragile by any means, but certainly haunted. "I must have asked myself that question a million times in the past fifteen years. The answer is always the same. I don't know."

"No professional guesses or hunches? No gut feeling?"

"Mostly just questions and I have plenty of those." He went to the refrigerator to survey the contents. "I'm a pretty basic cook," he warned as he reached for a carton of eggs.

Somehow Olive doubted he was basic at anything. She moved from the couch back to the bar so that she could watch his preparations. The motion of his hands mesmerized her as he chopped vegetables. Her gaze lingered on his battered knuckles as she imagined his fingers trailing along her backbone. She thought about their kiss that first night and wondered if the impulse would ever be repeated. Jack seemed more than content to keep her at arm's length. If that was a good thing, why did she suddenly feel so bereft?

She picked up her whiskey and sipped.

"Jack?"

"Yes?"

"I need to tell you something."

"I'm listening."

"It's about Anna."

The knife froze as he glanced up. He searched her face for the longest moment. "What about her?"

"I've heard something that you might not know. Maybe you don't want to know," Olive added.

He went back to his chopping. The blade sliced through the vegetables with studied precision. "Tell me."

"She used to work for Mona Sutton after school and sometimes on Saturdays."

"I remember. She wanted to be a psychologist."

"Yes, Mona said she was flattered at first that Anna wanted to follow in her footsteps, but after a while, she started to worry about Anna's motivation. She said it wasn't so much that Anna wanted to help people. She liked knowing things about them. Secrets."

Jack frowned. "What kind of secrets?"

"Mona wasn't specific, but she wondered if Anna had somehow accessed her files. She also told me about a hacking incident. Evidently, the school's whole system was compromised. Grades were changed. Scholarship applications were deleted. It would have been a real scandal if the district hadn't managed to keep it quiet. Mona thought Anna might have been involved. Did she ever say anything about it to you?"

Jack had gone very still. He seemed to drift away until the sizzle of butter in the frying pan brought him back. He lowered the heat and set the skillet aside. "I don't know anything about a hacking incident, but I did wonder about some of my grades. When I questioned a couple of the teachers, they claimed to have found mistakes. And there was one scholarship in particular that I never heard back from. The others were mostly rescinded after I became a suspect."

"That was so unfair to you."

He shrugged. "I don't know why Anna would have changed my grades, though. Let alone deleted scholarship applications."

"Maybe she didn't want you going away to school."

"She was going away herself." He grew pensive. "The one thing I could never figure out was motive."

"A motive for her murder, you mean? Do you think she found something incriminating in Mona's files? Something she used to blackmail another student? That seems out of character from what I remember of her."

"Anna was complicated."

"That's exactly what Mona said. I don't remember her that way at all, but then, I really didn't know her. I didn't know any of you very well, even my own cousin. But I find it hard to believe that a student could have a secret so dark he or she would be willing to kill to keep it from coming out."

"Who says it was a student?"

"I just assumed…" Olive trailed off as she watched him. "You have someone else in mind?"

"How well do you know Mona Sutton?"

"*Mona?* You can't be serious. What motive could she possibly have?"

"You said she suspected Anna had accessed her files. Maybe Anna found out something about her."

"Like what?"

Jack shrugged. "You tell me."

"This is pointless," Olive said with an irritated sigh. "We could sit here and build a case against anyone. It's easy when nothing more is required than idle speculation."

"Take it easy," Jack said.

"Sorry," she relented. "But Mona's a friend and Nathan is my cousin. I feel guilty talking about them behind their backs."

"We're just trying to find answers."

"Tie up those loose ends," she murmured.

In the ensuing silence, the coffeemaker started to drip, filling the cabin with a delectable aroma that reminded Olive of her mother, a true coffee connoisseur. She could drink cup after cup, but Olive wasn't so immune to caffeine. Coupled with the lingering adrenaline, she wondered if she would sleep a wink that night.

She glanced up from her drink to find Jack watching her. "What is it?"

"I was just wondering if you'd ever heard any rumors about Mona Sutton. An involvement with a student, anything like that?" His expression never altered, but Olive saw a flicker in his eyes that made her wonder.

She answered without hesitation. "No, never. Not so much as a whisper. Mona Sutton's reputation and behavior are exemplary."

"Doesn't it strike you as odd that someone with her credentials and education would choose to remain in a place like Pine Lake as a high school guidance counselor? The pay can't be that great."

Olive bristled. "Her salary is commensurate to mine. Which, you're right, isn't that great. But most of us don't do it for the money. We do it because we love our jobs and because what we do is important."

"I didn't mean to imply otherwise. I'm sorry if I offended you."

"I'm not offended. And, yes, I suppose I have wondered why someone like Mona would remain in Pine Lake. But she also has a private practice in addition to her work at school."

"I didn't know that."

"Now you do." Olive paused. "It's fine for the two of us to toss around conjecture in the privacy of this cabin, but a public accusation of this nature could ruin a career."

"Which is exactly my point," he said.

"Your point being that Anna may have found something on Mona Sutton. Possibly a relationship with a student. And the name of this student?"

"Tommy Driscoll."

Olive gaped. "You know this for a fact?"

"I don't know anything for a fact. As you said, this is nothing more than speculation in the privacy of my uncle's cabin. A conversation that will go no farther than the front door."

"Mona and Tommy." Olive shuddered. "I don't buy it. I just can't see it. She's a beautiful, sophisticated woman. Tommy Driscoll is…well, Tommy Driscoll. I suppose he's attractive in a good-old-boy kind of way and some might consider him charming, but he's always been so full of himself. So cocky."

And yet…

Hadn't she wondered herself why Mona had never married or even socialized in Pine Lake?

"Mona may have killed Anna because her relationship with a student was about to be exposed. That's your theory?"

"That's *a* theory," Jack said.

"I don't buy it."

"So you said."

"But now I'll never get that image out of my head. Thank you for that."

She saw a grin flash as he turned back to the stove.

He dished up the scrambled eggs, poured the coffee and they ate at the bar, choosing to discuss innocuous topics. Olive talked about her plans for the coming school year and her mother's recent marriage. Jack said little about his own life, but from the bits and pieces that she could cobble together, he seemed to lead a solitary existence. His parents had moved to Phoenix years ago and he had no siblings or cousins or anyone in his life he seemed close to. Undoubtedly his choice, but Olive sensed a restive nature that might always keep him discontent.

The meal concluded, she insisted on cleaning up while Jack went down to the dock to have a look around. She finished putting away the last of the dishes and then went outside to join him.

"You shouldn't be out here," he said. "It may not be safe."

"It may not be safe anywhere," she said with a shrug. "I've been thinking about that person on the bridge earlier. Why do you suppose he or she didn't wait until later to conduct a search? It was barely dark when I spotted the flashlight."

"Maybe he or she was afraid someone else would get there first."

Olive leaned her forearms against the rail, staring out over the water. Moonlight shimmered on the dark surface, reminding her of the fathomless mystery of Jack King's eyes. "First I was nearly run down by a truck that may or may not have been driven by Marc Waller. Then you were drugged and now I've been shot at it. What's going on in Pine Lake? What have we gotten ourselves into, Jack?"

"I don't know," he said in a strange tone. "But I'm sorry you got dragged into it."

"That's hardly your fault. I'm the one who climbed to the top of the bridge in my sleep, remember? I'm the one who was there when Jamie Butaud's body was thrown into the lake."

"I'm talking about tonight. I shouldn't have taken you with me."

She straightened. "If I'd stayed behind, whoever was on the bridge might have come looking for me here."

"No one knew you were at the cabin. Unless you told Nathan."

"I didn't. But aren't you forgetting someone? Beth knew."

"Yes." That odd note in his voice again.

"What if the cabin was being watched? What if I'm being watched? If Nathan figured out I was sleepwalking Monday night, maybe someone else has, too. Maybe the plan all along was to lure you away from the cabin."

"More maybes."

Olive glanced along the glimmering channel toward the bridge. The iron truss loomed dark and forbidding in the moonlight.

Slowly, she traced the shallow water, her gaze traveling the tree line and all along both banks. Nothing stirred. She saw nothing untoward in the darkness. No flickering lights, no furtive searching. The night was still, with the gentlest of breezes blowing across the water. And yet she had that same uncanny feeling she'd had earlier underneath the deck. Someone watched. Maybe from the bridge, maybe from the pine forest on the other side of the lake. Maybe even closer, from a boat hidden by a thick curtain of Spanish moss.

Someone watched.

Chapter Nine

Jack awakened with a start. A noise had roused him, but he couldn't say with any certainty what that sound had been.

He took a moment to orient himself to the darkness. He was in the bedroom of his uncle's cabin on Pine Lake. Olive lay sleeping in the living room, having insisted on taking the couch. Jack pushed himself up on his elbows, listening for a sign that she might be up stirring about, or worse, that an intruder was somewhere on the premises. A faint breeze drifted across the room, rippling the curtains at the window. Somewhere in the cabin, an outside door had been opened.

He rose from the bed and pulled on his jeans. Taking his weapon from the nightstand drawer, he left the room and slipped down the hallway to the living area. He checked the couch first. The covers lay crumpled and abandoned on the floor. The breeze tickled across his bare shoulders, drawing his gaze to the wall of windows that looked out on the deck. One of the glass doors stood slightly ajar.

He didn't think Olive would have left the cabin of her own accord, but she might not be cognizant of her actions. Tucking the gun in the back of his jeans, he went out on the deck. The moon was up, casting an eerie glow over the water as it shimmered down through the cypress trees. Across the lake, the pine forest loomed dark and impenetrable. Night sounds assailed him. The hoot of an owl. The forlorn cry of a loon.

An icy premonition stole down Jack's spine. Olive was somewhere out there alone, wandering the dark in her sleep while a killer lay in wait.

He left the deck and hurried down the steps to the dock. He hoped he might find her sitting in one of the chairs safe and sound, having slipped out of the cabin for a breath of fresh air. No such luck. He started to race back up the steps, but a flutter of movement out of the corner of his eye froze him. He turned slowly toward the water.

Olive was in the boat. Still dressed in the T-shirt he'd laid out for her earlier, she sat behind the wheel staring straight ahead. One hand rested on her bare leg as the other came up to trace along the instrument panel. She paused on the ignition. Then that hand also dropped to her lap and she remained motionless for the longest time until those furtive fingers came back up to search the dash.

Jack took a quick scan of their surroundings. The

dock lines had been unfastened. If not for a knot that had caught on one of the cleats, the boat would have drifted away.

"Olive?"

She didn't answer. She didn't acknowledge his presence with so much as a glance. Her fingers were still moving along the panel, pausing yet again on the ignition.

He knelt on the dock and pulled the boat back against the bumpers. Then he climbed down, steadying the rocking motion as best he could so that the movement didn't startle her awake. With her back to the lake, her face was a pale mask in the filtered moonlight, her eyes glassy and sightless. Gooseflesh prickled at Jack's nape.

"Olive," he called softly.

She gazed up at him and for a moment, Jack thought he must have roused her. But the eyes were blank, the hand moving along the dash unnervingly persistent.

"Can you hear me?" he asked.

"I need to go," she said.

Her expressionless voice sent another chill down his spine. "Go where?"

She stared out over the dock toward the bridge.

"Olive, you need to wake up." He waved a hand in front of her face. No reaction. Not even a blink.

She turned back to the wheel and the movement of her hand on the panel became more frenzied.

"Where do you need to go?" he asked again.

She didn't respond and Jack didn't know what to do. The last thing he wanted was to startle her awake. She could injure herself if she became frantic in such a small space and he might not be able to restrain her. But he certainly couldn't leave her here. It wasn't safe for either of them to be out in the open like this.

"Come on, Olive. Time to wake up." Taking her arm, he tried to gently ease her to her feet. He'd read somewhere that sleepwalkers were somewhat docile. Head them in the right direction and they would often go back to their beds. Olive wouldn't be budged.

He hunkered beside her, lowering his voice soothingly as he studied her profile. "Tell me where you need to go."

Once again she turned to stare out over the water.

"Are you trying to tell me you need to go back to the bridge? Why, Olive? Why the bridge?"

He thought about his earlier conversation with Nathan. The old lake bridge had once been important to Olive, a place she often retreated to after her father's tragic death. Maybe that was why she wanted to go there now. In some strange way, the bridge could still be a comfort to her. Or a punishment.

The frantic movement of her fingers along the panel seemed almost piteous to Jack now. He wanted to help her, calm her, but what he had in mind was risky and not altogether selfless. Olive had been wandering along Lake Side Road on the night of Anna's murder. What if she'd seen something before Nathan found her? What if those buried memories kept pulling her back to the bridge?

"Do you want me to take you there?" he asked.

No answer. She seemed oblivious to his presence, but when he eased her up from the seat, she willingly moved to the other side of the boat. Which seemed strange to Jack, and he wondered if a part of her brain was still cognizant.

He untangled the knot from the cleat and then fished in his pocket for the key. He had no idea if he was doing the right thing. He was in unfamiliar territory. Taking her to the bridge could be extremely dangerous. For all he knew, Jamie Butaud's murderer could still be prowling the darkness. But Jack had a gut feeling the situation could be even more perilous if he were to thwart Olive's compulsion. It was obvious that something important kept luring her back to the bridge.

The outboard rumbled to life, but the sound didn't faze her and Jack wondered if she'd been subconsciously braced for the roar. He placed one hand on the wheel and the other on the edge of his seat, ready to snatch her from danger if she started to get up, or worse, jump overboard. For now she sat motionless and stared straight ahead as he backed away from the dock and turned down the channel with only the moonlight to guide them.

The cypress trees were feathery against the pale light, the dripping Spanish moss undulant in a soft breeze. To his right, Jack could see the skeletal remains of a tree that had been struck by lightning. To his left, the glowing eyes of a night creature. Beside him, Olive sat silent as a ghost. An eerier trip Jack could hardly have imagined.

He found a place to put in near the bridge and hopped out, allowing the bow to run aground. He started to take Olive's arm but she was already climbing out, unmindful of his assistance. Her bare feet splashed in the water as she moved past him to the bank.

She went straight to the ladderlike support they had used two nights ago and Jack worried that she meant to climb to the top of the truss. He would have to stop her if she tried, but for now he stood nearby and let her take the lead.

For the longest time, Olive remained by the support, her head tilted skyward, as if she couldn't decide what to do. Then she turned and went up the bank to the deck. Jack followed at her side, guiding her away from the guardrail and around the treacherous spots in the floorboards.

Halfway across she paused to gaze out over the water. Then she turned to glance back at the bank as if she feared being followed. Satisfied, she fell to her knees and bent over the planks, trailing her hands all along the rough surface.

Jack knelt in front of her, mesmerized by the motion of her hands as they moved back and forth across the deck. She paused, hands hovering as she lifted her head, attracted by a night sound that only she could hear. Once again she cast a furtive glance over her shoulder before returning her attention to the floorboards.

Removing his phone from his pocket, Jack bent low, angling the flashlight beam along the deck beneath Olive's hands. What was she looking for? Or was she merely acting out some fragment of a long forgotten dream?

He trained the light straight down through the planks, expecting to see nothing but the distant glimmer of water. Instead, the beam sparked off something metallic wedged between the cracks of the floorboards. The tiny gold chain had fallen so deeply into the crevice and had been so thoroughly rooted in dirt and debris that it would never have been noticed if not for Olive's methodical searching.

The only tool Jack had with him was the boat key. He used the bit to dig down into the fissure until he could hook the chain over one of the teeth. Carefully, he fished the necklace up through the crack, catching his breath at the sight of the gold heart that dangled from a link. Despite fifteen years of dirt and grime, the embedded ruby—Anna's birthstone—still flashed with fire as the gemstone caught the moonlight.

Time had rendered the engraving on the back nearly illegible, but no matter. Jack remembered the simple inscription word for word: To Anna, from Jack. Love you always.

He'd given the necklace to her during their senior

year and she'd worn it every day until her death. He'd never known her to take it off. In hindsight, he wondered now if his choice of a heart had been his unwitting way of diminishing the significance of the one on her hip—the tattoo that had secretly labeled her as one of Tommy Driscoll's conquests.

Olive sat back on her heels, following the movement of the pendant as though under a hypnotist's spell. Then with a strange little sigh, she lay down on the bridge and closed her eyes, oblivious to her surroundings, oblivious to Jack, oblivious to the significance of her discovery.

OLIVE OPENED HER eyes to sunlight. She lay very still, staring up at the cedar plank ceiling as her heart thudded in panic. For a moment, she had no idea where she was. Had she sleepwalked into an unfamiliar bedroom?

Then bits and pieces of the previous night came back to her. Jack had talked her into staying at the cabin, which, to be truthful, hadn't been all that difficult after the events at the bridge. The last thing she'd wanted was to be alone in her unprotected house. Something sinister was going on in Pine Lake, and like it or not, she and Jack were in the middle of it. His growing list of suspects included Mona Sutton, a colleague and friend, and Nathan Bolt, the only remaining family Olive had left in this town.

For all she knew, she could be on Jack's list, too, although that seemed a reach. He'd given no indication that he was suspicious of her, but she needed to watch her step if for no other reason than to preserve her well-being. Her feelings for Jack King could easily get out of hand. An attraction was one thing, but she couldn't let herself fall in love with him. His stay in Pine Lake was transient and Olive knew from past experiences that she didn't handle loss well. Not real loss, the kind that hollowed out your insides and left you bereft. Three days ago, before Jack's return, she'd been perfectly happy with her life. Why rock the boat now—

Her thoughts splintered as she lifted up on her elbows and glanced around. Wait a minute. Why was she in the cabin's only bedroom? She'd insisted on taking the couch. She distinctly remembered watching the moon through the windows while she waited for sleep.

What had happened during the night? And why couldn't she remember? She hadn't had that much to drink, surely.

Swinging her legs over the side of the bed, she grabbed her clothes—neatly folded on a nearby chair—and padded down the hallway to the bathroom. After washing up and brushing her teeth, she dressed and followed the aroma of freshly brewed coffee out to the living area. Jack was in the kitchen fiddling with the coffeemaker. He turned when she came in and said good morning. Maybe it was Olive's imagination, but his greeting sounded stilted and he seemed to have a hard time meeting her gaze, making her wonder yet again about last night's events.

She went over and sat down on one of the barstools.

"Coffee?" he asked.

"Yes, please. Black and strong."

He poured a cup and set it before her. "How about some breakfast? I've got toast, cereal, fruit."

"No, thanks. I'm not much of a breakfast person. Coffee is fine."

He stood leaning against the counter, observing her as he folded his arms.

She put down her cup. "You're acting very strangely this morning so you may as well tell me what's wrong. Something happened last night, didn't it? I went to sleep on the couch and I woke up in the bedroom. I'd like to know why."

"You were sleepwalking," he said. "After I got you back inside, I thought it best that I take the couch so I'd awaken if you tried to leave the cabin again."

Icy fingers slid up her spine. "I left the cabin?"

He folded his arms as he gazed at her across the kitchen. "You really don't remember anything, do you?"

She frowned. "The last thing I remember is settling down on the couch."

"That's not entirely true," he said slowly.

Her scowl deepened. "What do you mean, it's not true? I would know if I remembered anything else."

"Would you? Are you sure about that?"

She said in exasperation, "Please stop dancing around the issue and tell me what happened last night."

"It's not just about last night, but that's a good place to start." He turned and poured himself a cup of coffee. "Let's go sit on the deck. I could use some air."

She reluctantly followed him outside, dreading what she might learn. If only they could sit in peace and quiet and enjoy the morning. It was early and the lake was lovely and calm. No voices, no cars, no ringtones. Just a fleeting moment of tranquility as the water lilies opened and the songbirds awakened.

Olive hated to shatter the zen-like stillness, but there was dark business to discuss. She turned to Jack, studying his profile as a breeze drifted across the deck, carrying the scent of the pines.

"I'm waiting," she said.

He took a gold chain from his shirt pocket, dangling it in the light before he closed his fist around it. "I woke up and you were gone," he said. "I found you down at the dock in the boat."

"What was I doing in the boat?"

"You'd tried to untie the lines, but a knot got caught on one of the cleats. Otherwise, you would have drifted away."

"I don't even remember leaving the cabin. What do you think I was doing in the boat?"

"You said you needed to go."

Her eyes widened. "I talked in my sleep?"

"Is that unusual?"

"Not for sleepwalking in general. Mumbles and moans are quite common, and some people have been known to carry on whole conservations without ever rousing. I don't think that's ever happened to me, though."

"How would you know unless someone told you?"

"I suppose that's true. So you found me in the boat…" she prompted.

"You were fiddling with the dash as if trying to start the ignition. And you kept gazing down the channel. It was obvious you meant to go back to the bridge. So I took you."

She stared at him in shock. "You took me back to the bridge? After someone shot at me there?"

"I know how that sounds." He looked momentarily chastised. "But it seemed important to you. Urgent, even. And I was with you the whole time. I never left your side for an instant. You've no reason to believe me, but I wouldn't let anything happen to you. Not then, not now."

Olive's breath quickened. His eyes were dark and deep and so piercing she could feel her armor crumbling. Quickly, she glanced away before he could see the alarm—and the longing—in her own gaze. "You don't owe me anything. You barely know me."

"It doesn't matter. I meant what I said."

Olive merely nodded because she didn't trust herself to speak at that moment. She didn't trust her resolve. It would probably be best for both of them if she got up and walked away. Kept her distance and her peace of mind. Instead, she sat there on Jack's deck, eyes fiercely focused on the water as her heart beat an uneasy rhythm inside her chest.

"To be honest, I had another reason for taking you to the bridge," he said. "I thought you might remember something."

"In my sleep?"

"I don't know how sleepwalking works. It seemed worth a shot. And my hunch paid off. Something did come back to you." He opened his fist, revealing the gold chain he'd taken out of his pocket earlier.

Olive noticed the heart pendant then and the flash of a tiny embedded ruby. She glanced up and found him watching her carefully. "*I* found it? Where?"

"It had fallen between the floorboards on the bridge. Impossible to see unless you knew where to look."

"May I?" She put out her hand. He seemed reluctant to relinquish the necklace at first, but then lifting his gaze to hers, he let the chain slip from his fingers into her palm.

The winking ruby enthralled Olive. The flash of fire awakened something in the deepest recesses of her consciousness. Not a memory. More like a lingering emotion from a forgotten dream.

"Do you recognize it?" Jack asked.

"I don't think so. But… I feel something when I look at it."

"What?"

The sharpness in his voice jolted her and the sensation fled. Her defenses came up as unease tickled across her scalp. "I don't understand. The necklace isn't mine. I don't remember having seen it before. And yet..." Her eyes closed briefly. "How could I have known where to find it on the bridge?"

"Look closely," he said. "Are you certain you don't recognize the charm?"

She held up the chain, allowing the heart to swing gently in the breeze. "From the way you're watching me, I assume you expect me to recognize it, but I don't. If I've seen it before, I can't remember where or when. Besides, a heart pendant is hardly an usual design."

"Turn it over and see if you can read the inscription."

Olive complied, furrowing her brow as she concentrated on the weatherworn engraving. Her hand trembled slightly as she glanced up. "This was Anna's?"

"She had it on the night she died."

Dread descended as Olive's heart started to hammer. "The necklace was wedged between the floorboards. Impossible to see unless one knew where to look, you said. If that's true, then I still don't understand how I happened upon it last night."

Jack leaned in, his gaze hard and relentless. "Because you were there the night Anna was killed. You must have seen the pendant fall from her neck. Or maybe the killer grabbed it from her throat. The point is, you saw where it lodged. You went straight to it last night. There's no way you could have known about Anna's necklace unless you witnessed her murder."

THE COLOR DRAINED from Olive's face. She looked vulnerable and yet somehow dauntless in her jeans and sneakers, with her hair still mussed from sleep and her blue eyes shadowed with fear.

For a moment the impulse to protect her was almost overpowering. Jack wanted nothing so much as to take her hand in his, pull her close and tell her that everything would be okay. He fought the urge to tuck back the strands of hair that curled in the breeze, to soothe away the worry lines that wrinkled her brow.

He wasn't a gallant man. Polite and respectful, yes, because he was still his mother's son, but he hadn't felt particularly chivalrous since his high school days. Olive Belmont had changed all that. From the moment their gazes had connected on top of that bridge, she'd made him feel things. Unexpected things. Unwanted things.

Complications, he reminded himself warily. He didn't need them.

She looked at him quizzically. "I don't suppose you believe in coincidences."

"Not in this case. You knew where to find that necklace, Olive. There's no getting around that."

She flinched. "But why did I only now remember? The pendant was wedged between those floorboards for fifteen years. And more to the point, why was someone else searching for it last night?"

"We don't know what that person was looking for. Something could have gotten left behind from Jamie Butaud's murder. But if the searcher really was looking for Anna's necklace, I can only assume my presence has created some anxiety. Here I am, back after all these years, and I'm asking a lot of unpleasant questions. Memories are stirring. Doubts are surfacing. Maybe that's why you remembered."

She glanced down at the chain pooled in her hand. "What are we going to do? This is evidence. We can't keep it to ourselves."

"That's exactly what we're going to do," Jack said. "This doesn't change anything. We already know Anna was on the bridge the night she died. The killer dumped her body in the water. The discovery of her necklace between the floorboards doesn't tell us anything about her death we didn't already know."

"Then there's no reason for the killer to worry. There's no reason why he would have been on the bridge last night."

"No reason that we know of. But the necklace does tell us something about you. If you saw what happened that night—"

"Don't." Olive turned with shadowed eyes. "I don't want to think about that. I don't want to think that this could have ended years ago if only I'd remembered. Maybe Jamie Butaud would still be alive."

"You can't think like that. For all we know, Jamie's murder is unrelated to Anna's."

"Do you really believe that?"

He thought about everything Nathan had told him the day before. Two young women murdered fifteen years apart, connected by the same tattoo that linked each of them to Tommy Driscoll. Jack didn't want to jump to conclusions, but at the very least, he needed to find out the county sheriff's whereabouts on the night of Jamie's murder.

"Jack?"

He glanced at Olive. She reached across the table and took his hand, placing the necklace gently in his palm and then closing her fingers around his. "You loved her very much, didn't you?"

"It was a long time ago. We were kids."

"Some things you don't get over."

The haunted look was back in her eyes and Jack thought again about his conversation with Nathan Bolt. Olive's dad had died in a terrible accident for which she blamed herself. Might still blame herself even after all these years. On the surface, she seemed like a happy woman, content and well adjusted. But deep down, she had secrets whether she remembered them or not.

She rose and went over to the railing to stare down at the dock. Jack hesitated for a moment and then got up to join her. The sun was up now, dappling the water lilies. The air was warm and redolent with the loamy scent of the lake.

Jack wished he had nothing more pressing than a day on the water with Olive, but a murderer was out there somewhere getting nervous and more dangerous by the minute.

"I should go," she said as if sensing his disquiet. "The security people are coming this morning and then I have to get to work. There's still so much to be done before school starts…" She trailed away into silence. "About that necklace…"

"What about it?"

She briefly touched the back of his hand. "I really don't remember ever having seen it. I'm not lying about that."

"I never thought you were."

"I know how much you want to solve Anna's murder. I'm sorry I can't be of more help."

He shrugged. "You've nothing to be sorry about. None of this is your fault. Not Anna's murder, not Jamie's, any of it."

"Yes, but what if I do have hidden memories of that night? I can't help but wonder how your life might have been changed if only I'd remembered what happened."

"Maybe I like my life just fine the way it is."

"You almost sound convincing."

He straightened, gazing down at her with a pensive frown. "You carry a lot of guilt on your shoulders, don't you?"

She smiled. "It's kind of my thing. And yours is downplaying your feelings. I know how deeply you loved Anna. I could see it on your face every time you looked at her. I used to wonder what it would be like to have someone look at me like that. Sometimes I still wonder." Her tone was self-deprecating but her smile turned wistful.

That smile did things to Jack. The dreaminess. The open yearning.

He scowled at the sparkling water as his restlessness edged into an unexpected longing. "I'll always grieve for what might have been, but for Anna's sake, not mine. She deserved a long and happy life. But I haven't been carrying a torch for her all these years. I'm not still in love with a dead girl." He turned. "Anna's ghost doesn't haunt me, Olive. And her memory has nothing to do with how I feel about you."

He heard her breath catch. Her eyes were very blue as she stared up at him. Clear and yet somehow unfathomable. Earnest and yet deeply guarded. "How do you feel about me?" she asked on a near whisper.

He didn't answer. Instead he reached out and smoothed back her hair, letting his fingers tangle in the russet strands as their gazes clung. If Jack had sensed even the slightest resistance, he would have let the moment slip away. But Olive didn't contest, just the opposite. She leaned in, her lips slightly parted, her eyes hooded and sultry. He stared down at her for another moment before he cupped her neck and pulled her to him.

The kiss was slow and testing, without the sponta-

neity and adrenaline of their first. And yet the impact
rocked Jack to his core. He drew back, searching her
face before he bent and kissed her again, this time
wrapping his arms around her waist and lifting her
so that they were face to face, mouth to mouth, heartbeat to heartbeat. She weighed nothing. So slight
she could have easily slipped from his arms and so
he tightened his embrace as he deepened the kiss.

Desire flared. Hot and quick. He wanted her then
and there, on the deck, in the open, with the leaves
whispering all around them and the songbirds looking down from the treetops. He wanted her writhing
and ready as the swamp teemed with a primal awakening. But he held back because there was something
else in that kiss, too. Deeper, darker, more complicated emotions.

Whether she sensed his hesitation or had her
own reservations, he would never be certain, but
she pulled away, staring into his eyes as she slid back
to the deck. She lifted her fingers to her lips as if she
could somehow capture their kiss.

"That was…unexpected."

"Was it?"

She shivered. "Maybe not. Jack?"

"Yes?"

"You never answered my question."

"I think I did. Eloquently, I would hope."

She laughed softly as she turned to stare out over
the lake, squinting as a shaft of sunlight bounced
off the water. "This—whatever this is…" She made

a gesture between them, connecting them. "It isn't going to end well, is it?"

"Probably not."

"But that's not going to stop us."

"No."

She tracked an egret skimming the water before turning back to him with a nod. "Okay," she said. "But just so you know, my eyes are wide open."

Chapter Ten

Olive propped an elbow on her desk and cradled her chin in her palm. Worry and caffeine had given her a headache and she felt apathetic about the million and one things left to do on her agenda. A week ago, all she could think about was excelling in her new position and proving herself to a seemingly dubious school board, but her priorities had suddenly shifted.

It wasn't just her attraction to Jack King that occupied her thoughts. In fact, she was trying her best *not* to think about those feelings or that kiss. There would be time enough later to overanalyze every nuance. Right now, however, Olive had more pressing problems. In the space of one short night, she'd been shot at by an unknown gunman and had recovered Anna Grayson's long-lost necklace. A necklace Anna had been wearing on the night of her murder.

That Olive had apparently witnessed something didn't bode well for her peace of mind or her physical safety. Jack had promised to do everything in his power to protect her, but could she trust him to have her best interests at heart? He also had an agenda. He had come back to Pine Lake to solve Anna's murder and now that he knew Olive was a material witness, how far would he go to try and recover her memories?

Ever since Jamie Butaud's body had been found, Olive had worried that she might have seen something from the top of the lake bridge, that the identity of Jamie's killer might be hidden somewhere in her subconscious, waiting for a trigger to release it. But she'd never considered the possibility that she had witnessed *Anna Grayson's* murder. In fifteen years, not a single clue had surfaced until last night.

But Jack was right. How else could she have known where to look for that necklace? Why else would she have gone in search of it in her sleep?

What else might be locked in her subconscious?

On the surface, it seemed like too much of a coincidence that she could have been an unwitting witness to two brutal slayings, but her presence on the bridge on the night of Anna's murder hadn't been happenstance. After her family's move to Pine Lake, Olive had gone to the bridge to wallow in her guilt and to grieve for her dad. The place had become a haven for her and eventually a habit. From everything she knew about her disorder, a sleepwalker often repeated everyday behavior. Going to the bathroom. Getting a drink of water. Climbing to the top of the old lake bridge.

Her fixation on the structure could explain her

presence fifteen years ago, but what about on Monday night? What had brought back the falling dreams and her sleepwalking trip to that bridge?

At first, Olive had chalked up her restless slumber to the anxiety and uncertainty of a new job, but now she wondered if she had been picking up on subtle clues and vibes from the people around her. The people on Jack's list. Mona and Nathan and Tommy Driscoll.

After all, her first close call had come before Jamie's death, before Jack's arrival in Pine Lake. A dark sedan had come out of nowhere last Friday night to send Olive scrambling for the curb. She'd been certain that one or more malicious students had wanted to intimidate her, but in light of recent events, the intent was undoubtedly darker.

Nathan had suggested that Marc Waller was targeting Olive as a means to get to him, but had Marc really been that resentful of Nathan's relationship with Jamie or was there another reason for the bad blood between them? It didn't make sense to Olive and yet she could think of no other reason why she had ended up in Marc Waller's crosshairs. She barely knew him and had had little contact with Jamie since the troubled girl had dropped out of high school.

It pained Olive to think that the power to bring a killer to justice had been within her grasp all along if only she could remember. She could have ended Jack's misery years ago and given closure to Anna's family. The whole town could have healed. And Jamie Butaud might still be alive.

Pointless to blame herself, of course, but Jack was right about that, too. Olive was a master at taking on irrational guilt. She wasn't culpable for what had happened to Anna Grayson or Jamie Butaud any more than she was responsible for her dad's accident. But that hadn't stopped her from agonizing over what might have been. Olive had begged her dad to drive home that night even though she knew the roads were treacherous. She'd been selfish and thoughtless and petulant, but she had also been a kid. She'd eventually forgiven herself, but every now and then, the what-ifs caught up with her. Like now.

She swiveled her chair around to stare out the window, using the slow drift of cumulous clouds against the vivid blue sky to lull her into a meditative state. It was hot and steamy outside, but Olive sat shivering in her air-conditioned office. Maybe if she could conjure up one memory, the rest would fall like dominos. But was that even a good idea? Anna's killer had gone free all these years and if Olive was the only one who could identify him—

She whirled as a noise outside her office startled her. The school was old and full of strange sounds. She told herself to relax. She was hardly alone. In these final weeks, teachers were in and out of the building as they prepared their classrooms and curriculum. The custodial workers and support staff were also hard at work. There was nothing at all to be concerned about. Except...

The sound had seemed furtive somehow. Clandestine footsteps retreating through the reception area.

Olive rose silently and crossed her office to peer through the glass panel. No one was in the outer office. The administrative assistant had gone out for an early lunch and then a doctor's appointment. She wouldn't be back until midafternoon, but others were surely about. All Olive had to do was step into the hallway and she would undoubtedly find someone working in one of the other offices.

She crossed the reception area and once again paused to stare through the window. Then she opened the door and slipped into the corridor glancing both ways in apprehension. Nothing was amiss. No one stirred. And yet Olive had the discomfiting feeling that something was wrong.

Hugging the wall, she made her way down the hallway, checking for signs of life. The empty classrooms seemed to mock her and more than once, she paused to glance over her shoulder. Olive had spent most of her life in academic settings of one level or another. She found comfort in the musty mingle of textbooks, chalkboards and lockers. But there had always been something spooky about a deserted school building. Lingering emotions seemed to echo through the hallways and down the stairwells.

She'd dressed for comfort that morning in slim black pants and a blue knit top. The soft soles of her ballet flats hushed her footfalls on the tile floor as she approached the stairs and glanced over the railing. She took a deep breath and called out in what she hoped was a nonchalant voice. "Hello? Anyone down there?"

The question bounced off the walls and came right back to her. She waited for a response, hoping to hear a good-natured rejoinder from one of the teachers. Instead she was greeted by a weighty silence.

"Hello?" she called down again. The word ricocheted back to her. *Hello. Hello. Hello.*

She turned and retraced her footsteps down the hallway, pausing to peek inside the teachers' lounge. Empty. As were all the nearby classrooms. This was very unusual. Almost as if it had been planned. Olive didn't want to give in to the crazy notion of a conspiracy, but where was everyone?

Mona Sutton's office was located across the corridor and up a short flight of stairs. Olive had never thought about it before, but the elevation of the guidance counselor's office had the effect of isolating Mona from the student body. Olive had an image of the cool blonde hovering on her private landing, observing the students from afar, taking in things that no one else would notice. *I saw the way you looked at him when you passed in the hallway. And all those shy glances from your locker.*

The door was closed and Olive couldn't see a light or any movement behind the frosted glass panel. She started to retreat to her own office when she heard a metallic clank followed by a muted oath.

Nothing to worry about. Mona was undoubtedly busy with her own preparations for the coming school year. Perhaps she was going through her file cabinets, which would explain the noise. It did not explain the voices, however, one deep and angry and unmistakably male.

Another teacher, perhaps. Or someone from the cleaning staff.

Olive tried to remain calm, reminding herself sternly that there was likely an innocent explanation for the muffled commotion and yet everything inside her stilled as her instincts screamed another warning. She wavered indecisively. She could climb the stairs and barge through the door to confront whoever was inside. Or she could go in search of a teacher or custodian to accompany her. She could even call the police. The school was located well within the city limits so she wouldn't have to deal with Tommy Driscoll. But if Mona was inside the office and Olive had panicked for no reason, word would get out about her irrational behavior. Her credibility—never mind her authority—would be undermined. If she overreacted at the slightest noise, how would she handle a real crisis?

To be fair, she had every right to be cautious. Considering the events of the previous evening, she would be crazy not to be careful.

Drawing a breath, she tried to rein in her panic as

she moved across the hallway and paused at the bottom of the steps. No sound came to her now, but she had an unnerving premonition that someone was on the other side of the door listening for her approach.

Even a week ago, Olive wouldn't have hesitated to bound up the stairs and knock on the door or even to call out to Mona. But Jack's suspicions had rubbed off on her and she found herself conjuring an unwanted image. Mona's fingers sliding around Anna Grayson's neck, squeezing and squeezing until—

Olive's gaze remained fixed on the frosted glance panel as she moved up the steps. A shadow hovered on the other side of the door. Not her imagination. She put a hand on the latch, still unsure what to do when the door was yanked back and she found herself face to face with Mona Sutton. It was the first time Olive had seen Mona since Jack had sown those seeds of doubt and now Olive found herself jumping at the sudden confrontation, her hand flying to her heart in alarm.

The guidance counselor looked uncharacteristically disheveled with tendrils frizzing from her normally sleek bun and her signature ruby lipstick worn thin. She recovered so quickly Olive almost wondered if she had imagined the high color in the woman's cheeks and the feverish gleam in her eyes.

"Olive? What on earth…?"

"You startled me," she said on a breath. "I wasn't expecting to see you."

"Wasn't expecting to see me? This is my office

last time I checked." In one fluid motion, Mona smoothed back her hair as she planted herself in front of the door, blocking Olive's view inside the office. Again, those insidious seeds took root and Olive found herself trying to catch a glimpse over Mona's shoulder.

"I didn't think you were in today," Olive said lamely. "I heard a noise—voices, actually—and I half convinced myself that someone had broken into your office. I couldn't see a light and so I thought…" She gave an awkward laugh. "I know that sounds crazy."

Mona said in a stilted voice, "I was just doing some housekeeping. As for voices, I had a podcast on in the background." The plausible explanation flowed from her lips as she took in Olive's distressed demeanor. "You really do look shaken. Are you okay?"

"Too much caffeine and not enough sleep," Olive said with a shrug. "But now that I'm here, do you have a minute?"

"Of course." Mona pulled the door closed. "I was just on my way out. Do you mind if we walk and talk?"

"That's…fine."

They went down the steps together. The building was silent except for their footfalls, but Olive could have sworn someone remained in the office. She had to resist the urge to glance over her shoulder.

As if sensing her disquiet, Mona took her arm. "What's wrong? You still seem upset."

"I can't stop thinking about what happened to Jamie Butaud."

Mona sighed. "Nor can I. The whole town is on edge. It's all anyone can talk about."

"Can you blame them?" Olive cast an uneasy glance down the hallway. "Another murder, another killer out there roaming free." Or inside the school building.

Stop it!

Speculation was one thing, but now she was allowing her imagination to run amok. She and Mona Sutton had been friends and colleagues for years. Nothing had changed between them except for Jack King's innuendos.

But that noise in Mona's office. The male voice. Her flustered demeanor and reluctance to allow Olive a glimpse inside…

"It's very unsettling," Mona said.

"Very." Olive ran a hand up and down her chilled arm. "Speaking of unsettling—have you noticed how quiet the building is today? Where is everyone?"

"People are around. I bumped into Beth Driscoll earlier. She was downstairs in the science lab."

"How did she seem?" Olive asked carefully.

Mona's brows lifted. "That's an odd question. She seemed fine. On edge like the rest of us, but coping. Why would you be concerned about Beth?"

Because Jack planted the outrageous notion in my head that you had an affair with her husband when he was still a student, giving you both a motive for Anna's murder.

Olive cleared her throat. "I'm concerned about all the staff. As you said, everyone is on edge."

Mona lowered her voice as she leaned in. "Just between you and me, you've every right to be concerned about Beth Driscoll. It's hardly a secret that she was hoping to be appointed principal. Being passed over must have been a slap in the face. That kind of resentment doesn't go away overnight."

"I had no idea," Olive said, her stomach churning at the thought of conflict in the ranks even before school started.

"Oh, come on," Mona chided. "You must have heard all the grumbling when the announcement was made. Beth even threatened to tender her resignation."

"I knew there would be hard feelings, but I didn't realize the extent of the dissension. Maybe I didn't want to."

"I wouldn't have brought it up, but you asked about Beth." Mona gave her a brief smile. "Anyway, it's settled business. You're the new principal and it's time for everyone to accept your promotion and move on."

Olive thought that everyone had accepted her. The meeting on Tuesday had gone more smoothly than she could have hoped and when she and Beth had spoken at the dock, the science teacher had seemed eager to discuss the coming school year. Had her magnanimous congratulations disguised a simmering resentment? What else might Beth Driscoll be hiding?

"Olive?"

She jumped as her gaze and attention darted back to Mona.

"You really are jittery today, aren't you?"

She smoothed a hand down her pants leg. "Sorry."

Mona gave her a curious evaluation. "You said you haven't been sleeping well. What else is going on with you?"

Olive paused. "I keep thinking about our last conversation. What you said about Anna Grayson's penchant for secrets and your suspicion that she may have accessed your records."

"It was only a suspicion. I never had any real proof."

"For the sake of argument, let's say she did. Do you think it's possible she found something in your files that led to her death?"

"What do you mean?"

"A secret," Olive said. "One so dire that someone was willing to kill to keep it quiet."

Mona frowned. "You know I can't talk about the content of my files."

"Even if it could help bring a killer to justice?"

"Even then." A moment passed before she continued. "Aren't you forgetting something? A man was tried, convicted and is now serving life in prison for Anna Grayson's murder."

"What if they got the wrong man?"

Mona's tone turned mildly reproachful. "You think Wayne Foukes is innocent? Despite his criminal record? Despite his lack of an alibi? Despite Anna's ring being found in his possession?"

"Yes, despite all that. I've always had my doubts."

"Really? Because it seems to me those doubts only surfaced when Jack King came back to town."

"That's not true," Olive defended. "I do have a mind of my own, you know."

Mona's expression grew troubled. "A word to the wise?"

"Of course."

"Watch yourself, Olive. You've got a lot at stake and this year will be difficult enough without all these outside distractions. I know you have a tendency to jump into causes with both feet, but you need to be careful with Jack King. He's been gone from Pine Lake for a very long time. How much do any of us really know about him anymore?"

"How much do we really know about each other?" Olive countered.

That seemed to give Mona pause. She looked as if she wanted to argue, but then she acquiesced with a shrug. "You have a point. But I can't help worrying about his influence on you, especially considering his background. Do you know anything about his life in Houston? About the outfit he works for?"

Very little, Olive realized. "He's in private security."

"The Blackthorn Agency is more than a private

security firm. It's a worldwide operation with a reputation that's questionable at best. The owner, Ezra Blackthorn, is rumored to be ex-CIA. His employees, including Jack, are former military and law enforcement officers with seemingly one thing in common—they're all basically misfits and malcontents."

Olive stared at her in shock. "How can you possibly know that?"

Another pause. "I saw Tommy Driscoll earlier. He seems to know quite a lot about the Blackthorn Agency."

"As if I would trust his word about anything," Olive said coolly. She couldn't resist turning to glance behind her. They were out of sight of Mona's office, but she wondered again about that male voice, angry and muted. About Mona's unkempt appearance. "Where did you see him?"

"He was here looking for Beth."

Olive searched her face for a telltale twitch or flinch. Nothing in Mona's deportment gave her away and yet Olive could have sworn she saw something dark swirling in the woman's eyes. "I thought you said Beth is downstairs working in the science lab."

"She was there earlier, but she must have skipped out after I bumped into her. Tommy couldn't find her. She wasn't answering her phone and with everything that's happened, I guess he got worried. Anyway, we talked for a bit and Jack's name came up. Apparently, the sheriff's office has been looking into his background."

"Why?"

"*Why?* Because a young woman was murdered on the night of his return."

Olive was outraged. "But Jack didn't even know Jamie Butaud. And he's the one who discovered the body, for crying out loud."

"I'm sure the background check is just routine," Mona said with a placating smile.

But Olive was far from pacified. "What else did Tommy say? Tell me the truth. Is Jack a suspect? Is that the reason for your concern?"

Mona looked offended by the question. "Our friendship is the reason for my concern. And I don't need Tommy Driscoll or anyone else to tell me that Jack King is a dangerous man."

BETH DRISCOLL STOOD on the old lake bridge staring down into the water. Sunlight shimmered in her dark hair as a mild breeze billowed the skirt of her yellow dress. On first glance, her stance seemed casual, but as Jack closed the distance between them, he was struck by the intensity of her focus and the way her hands gripped the iron railing so tightly her knuckles had whitened. She seemed a million miles away, completely unaware of his presence. The day was already hot and humid, but he couldn't dispel a sudden chill as he moved up beside her.

"Beth?"

She turned slowly as if taking her time to come back from wherever her mind had wandered. "Jack?"

She dropped her hands from the guardrail, tucking them into the pockets of her dress as she gave him a tentative smile. "What are you doing here?"

"I was about to ask you the same thing." He couldn't help but notice the dark circles beneath her eyes and the deep furrows in her brow—physical manifestations of a deeply distressed woman. "Are you okay?"

A veil dropped over her expression. "Yes, why?"

He shrugged. "You seemed pretty tense when I came up just now."

"Oh, I was just daydreaming. Don't tell anyone you saw me, okay? I'm playing hooky." Her tone was light, but something hard glinted in her eyes.

"Your secret is safe with me." The breeze stirred her perfume, a light, floral fragrance with a darker trace of musk. The dichotomy of the notes seemed symbolic of two disparate personalities, and Jack was struck once again by the notion of a night and day Beth Driscoll.

"I always liked coming to this bridge." She swept her gaze along the railing where the remnant of a crime scene tape fluttered in the breeze. "I know that must sound a little insensitive considering everything that's happened, but my memories of this place aren't all bad. We had some good times here, didn't we? All those parties. The midnight swims."

"We had some good times," he agreed.

She tucked back her hair as she gave him a curious appraisal. "So what brings you here this morning?"

He lowered his gaze to the deck as an image came back to him—Olive with glazed eyes and a blank expression kneeling on the floorboards, searching and searching along the planks.

"I thought I'd have a look around," he said. "Someone was on the bridge last night. I spotted a flashlight beam moving around in the dark. I think whoever was up here was looking for something."

Beth glanced at him in alarm. "Did you see who it was?"

"No, I never got a good look."

Was that relief that flashed in her eyes?

"What do you think they were looking for?" she asked worriedly.

"That's what I'm trying to figure out."

She put a hand on the guardrail as if steadying herself against the subtle sway of the truss. Did she know who had been here the night before? Or did she at least suspect?

Jack studied her features, taking note of those shadowed eyes and the wasted lines of her body beneath the thin cotton of her dress. As if all too aware of his scrutiny, she folded her arms and shivered. "Whatever they were looking for, do you think it had something to do with Jamie Butaud's murder?"

"I don't know," he said truthfully. "But it's been my experience that even with the best-laid plans, something always gets overlooked. Something always gets left behind."

She shook her head. "You really don't give up, do you?"

"To the contrary, some might say I have a habit of giving up too easily."

A frown flitted. "I find that hard to believe. You seem dedicated to a fault."

"To a fault, huh?" He rested his forearms on the guardrail as he gazed down into the water. The sun was hot on his back, but an indefinable chill still gripped him. Beth Driscoll had triggered an alarm, but Jack didn't yet know why. "If I were as committed as you seem to think, I wouldn't have left town the way I did. I would have stayed and fought to clear my name. I would have done everything in my power to make sure justice was served."

"You're too hard on yourself. No one can fault you for leaving Pine Lake. Some days I wonder why any of us stayed."

Jack straightened. "Why *did* you stay?"

"The obvious reason. I was in love. Or thought I was. Back then, Tommy Driscoll was my whole world."

"And now?"

She was silent for a long moment. "Let's just say, Jamie's death has brought back a lot of painful memories. For all of us, I suspect. And now here you are in Pine Lake and it's a little too easy to dwell on what might have been."

What caused that glint in her eyes? Jack wondered. What secrets lurked behind her reluctant smile? "You're young," he said. "Why dwell on what might have been when you have your whole life ahead of you? You can still leave Pine Lake. You can do whatever you want."

Her smile turned wan. "You make it sound so easy, but I'm not brave enough to start over. It's easier to accept what I have and pretend it's enough."

The fatalistic note might have stirred Jack's sympathy if not for that strange gleam in her eyes. He still couldn't dismiss the notion that there was more to Beth Driscoll than he'd ever considered. She seemed both deeper and darker than the girl he remembered from high school. He was starting to wonder if his devotion to Anna had blinded him to the complicated nature of those around him. Including Anna.

"Beth?"

She turned.

"I need to ask you something." He watched her carefully as she nodded. "Where were you the night Anna was murdered?"

She looked stunned. "What? *Jack.* You can't be serious."

"We all left the stadium together after the game. I took Anna home early because she said she didn't feel well. Tommy ended up at Nathan's house, but where were you? Why weren't the two of you together that night?"

She ran a finger along the railing. "We had a fight.

I don't remember what it was about. Probably a girl. There were a lot of those fights." She glanced at him coyly. "There were a lot of those girls."

"And yet you stayed with him."

"He always came back to me."

"Did you ever fight about Anna?"

Her voice sharpened. "Why would we fight about Anna?"

"You knew about them, didn't you?"

She looked on the verge of denial. Emotions warred in her eyes before her lips thinned and she turned away with a sigh. "I didn't know, but I suspected."

"What aroused your suspicion?" Jack asked.

"I could always tell." Her eyes closed briefly. "With Anna, it was the little things. The way he looked at her. The way she wouldn't look at him."

"You didn't confront them?"

"No." She shrugged. "I guess I didn't want my worst fears confirmed. I thought Tommy was the love of my life and Anna was my best friend. My *best* friend. I confided in her about the pregnancy, about my decision to keep the baby, *everything*." Her hands clenched into fists at her sides. "I was angry with her. You've no idea. I felt betrayed. So helpless and *small*. I just wanted to curl up somewhere and die. I wanted her to die, too, but I didn't kill her. I swear it." She drew a shaky breath. "God, Jack. Say something. *Please*. Don't just stand there staring at me like that."

"I'm still trying to put it all together," he said slowly.

She ran fingers through her ruffled hair. "Put what together? I told you everything. But now you doubt me. I can see it in your eyes."

Jack took a moment before he answered. "Why did you try so hard to convince me of Anna's faithfulness when we spoke on the dock yesterday? Why didn't you just tell me the truth?"

She flung out her hands in supplication. "I didn't want to hurt you. What purpose would that truth serve after all these years? And maybe a part of me still wanted to deny it."

"You should have told me, Beth. This was information I needed a long time ago."

Her eyes flashed with subtle defiance. "Why? Because their betrayal gave me a motive for Anna's murder? It gave you one, too, Jack. Did you consider that?"

"Are you saying you kept silent to protect *me*?"

"Think about it for a minute. In all those months of persecution, the sheriff could never come up with a reason you'd wanted Anna dead. You had means and opportunity, but no motive."

"Your silence didn't just protect me, though, did it, Beth? Or you, for that matter. It kept hidden a link between Tommy and Anna."

She said nothing to that.

"Did he ever tell you where he was that night?" Jack pressed.

"You said yourself he was at Nathan's."

"According to Nathan, Tommy left at some point, supposedly to meet a woman, possibly a teacher. Did you suspect that relationship, too?"

She didn't rise to his bait. She remained cool and almost unnaturally calm. "I wouldn't put too much stock in what Nathan Bolt says. He and Tommy had a falling out years ago and Nathan has been vindictive ever since. Even before that really. Remember how obnoxious and competitive he was in school? Especially with you. He couldn't stand that you had it all—looks, brains, athleticism. He had to trade exclusively on his intellect, and his grades didn't always reflect how smart he claimed to be."

"Are you suggesting he killed Anna to get back at me?"

"You lost all those scholarships, didn't you? You became the town pariah. You think Nathan didn't secretly enjoy every minute of your misery? He wasn't a good person. Not then, not now. Anna couldn't stand him."

"She never told me she had a problem with Nathan."

Beth gave him a sidelong glance. "It seems she didn't tell you a lot of things."

Now it was Jack who refused to rise to the bait.

She smiled at his silence. "Isn't it funny the way things turned out? You and Anna were the golden couple. Everyone thought you had this grand, fairy-tale romance. Yet Tommy and I are the ones who stayed together."

Was that something she really wanted to throw in his face? Jack wondered.

She cocked her head, giving him a long assessment. "Can I ask *you* something? What's going on between you and Olive Belmont?"

Another alarm sounded, but Jack merely shrugged. "What makes you think something is going on?"

"I'm not blind. I've seen you together and I'm still very adept at reading people. The way you looked at her—the way she looked at you. There was a lot of tension on that dock yesterday. I just can't help wondering why *her*, of all people?"

Of all people? The question grated and Jack frowned. "Do you have a problem with Olive?"

"A problem? No. I just never would have pegged her as your type."

He didn't at all like the direction of this conversation. He didn't trust Beth Driscoll and he braced himself for what she might be up to. "How would you know my type?"

"I know Olive. We've worked together for several years now and I've always found her to be more than a little eccentric."

"Is that a bad thing?"

"Not necessarily but when you put it together with her behavior in high school…" She shrugged. "Don't you remember the way she followed us around all the time? The way she *watched* us."

"She was just a shy kid," Jack said. "I don't remember her ever saying two words to any of us."

"She was only three years younger than we were. Old enough to have a serious crush on you, Jack. It couldn't have been more obvious."

"Why are you telling me this?"

She lifted a thin shoulder as she turned back to the water. "I don't know. I guess I thought you'd want to know. Maybe I thought you needed to know."

Her pensive profile brought back a memory—not of Olive—but of Beth standing at that very rail in a shooter's stance firing at a row of tin cans that Tommy had lined up on a log. Then another image danced into focus, the X-shaped exit wound in Jamie Butaud's forehead.

As if sensing the direction of his thoughts, Beth said abruptly, "I should be getting back before Tommy sends out a search party." She placed a hand on Jack's arm. His first extinct was to shrink away from her touch. "You take care while you're in town, Jack. This is not a good place."

Was that a subtle warning he heard in her voice?

He watched her walk away, hands at her sides, head slightly bowed. When she got to the end of the bridge, she paused and glanced over her shoulder. She held his gaze for the longest moment and then she was gone, swallowed up by the deep shadows cast by the piney woods.

But a chill lingered and an omen niggled as Jack pondered the mystery of Beth Driscoll.

Chapter Eleven

"I had a disturbing encounter this morning," Olive said as she and Jack stood on the dock enjoying a late afternoon drink.

"I had a pretty strange morning myself," he said.

"Oh?"

"You go first."

Olive nodded, but her mind had already started to wander. She'd never considered herself the flighty type—if anything, she was usually a little too rigid and structured—but Jack's proximity threw her. She couldn't organize her thoughts. She couldn't concentrate on anything but the ruffle of his hair in the breeze and the sexy scruff that shadowed his jaw and chin.

Olive had gone straight home after work to shower and change, and her plan had been to settle in with her latest budget projections. But she'd soon grown restless and had gone out for a short stroll. A call from Jack had brought her all the way down to the lake. With every step she took, she'd told herself to turn back, to take this thing between them no farther. But here she was. Here *he* was.

They were both dressed casually for a relaxed evening on the water, but Olive was far from calm and collected. She was too acutely aware of the man beside her, too intensely aware of their last conversation.

She sipped her drink as she gave him a stealthy perusal. He had on sunglasses, which hid his expression so she fixated instead on his mouth. The tiny crease in the center of his bottom lip fascinated her. She studied the anomaly for a moment before trailing her gaze along his jawline, across his shoulders and all the way down his tanned arms to his hands, one of which was wrapped tightly with gauze and tape. The stark evidence of his memory loss gave her only a moment's hesitation as she imagined those long fingers slipping down the small of her back, easing over her hips, gliding along the inside of her thighs…

Drawing a quick breath, she forced her attention back to the lake. The shadows cast by the pine forest crept slowly across the water, but the dock was still bathed in sunlight. Olive lifted her ponytail, allowing the breeze to cool the back of her neck as she watched a heron step daintily into the shallow water.

"Are you going to finish that story?" Jack prompted. "You had a disturbing encounter…?"

"Oh, right. I was working in my office on the second floor. The building was very quiet. My assistant had gone out for lunch and I had the whole place to myself. I don't know if you've ever been in an old school building alone, but it has a strange vibe. More so at night, but even in broad daylight, it can be unsettling with all those odd sounds and old memories that seem to echo through the hallways." She hesitated. "Does that sound crazy?"

"No, I'm with you. Odd sounds, old memories…"

"Yes, well, it started to get to me. A feeling came over me that I was being watched. The sensation was so strong, in fact, that I left my office to investigate."

Jack's voice sharpened. "Why didn't you call me?"

"Because I hoped it was just my imagination. But I've been experiencing that same sensation for a few days now. I chalked it up to being nervous about my new job and the coming school year. I tend to be a worrywart and I'm sometimes prone to panic."

"You were steady as a rock behind the wheel of the boat," he commented.

She smiled. "On the surface, maybe. Anyway, everything seemed fine at first. Then I heard a noise coming from Mona Sutton's office. The sound was metallic, like someone banging into a desk or closing a file drawer. And I heard voices, one of them male. They were arguing."

"Did you recognize the voices?"

"No, and by that time, my imagination really had gotten the better of me. I became convinced that someone had broken into Mona's office to search through her files. Maybe even to destroy evidence."

"Of what?"

Olive gave him a wide-eyed stare. "Murder, of course."

He lifted a brow. "So you thought it a good idea to check things out on your own?"

"Well…yes. When I got to the top of the stairs, the door burst open and there was Mona, looking all flushed and disheveled. I don't know how well you remember her, but Mona Sutton never looks anything other than perfect. And the way she so abruptly threw open the door made me wonder if she'd heard my footsteps on the stairs and wanted to head me off. She even stepped in front of the doorway to make certain I couldn't see into her office. I kept picturing Tommy Driscoll inside, the two of them *in flagrante delicto*. You put that image in my head," she accused. "You've made me very suspicious."

"You say that like it's a bad thing."

"It is," she insisted. "It's one thing to be cautious, but I hate thinking the worst of my friends and colleagues. I saw it coming, though. That morning in front of the coffee shop…the way you said *these people*… I knew things would get ugly once you started asking questions. Suspicions would flare. People would start to doubt one another. It's already started. I experienced it firsthand this morning with Mona. She tried very hard to convince me that you're a dangerous man, Jack."

His lowered voice raised goose bumps along her arms. "What do you think?"

Olive's heart thudded as she gazed into those dark glasses. She couldn't see his expression, but she could feel the intensity of his stare. It made her feel anxious and excited and wary. She gripped the railing. "I think we need to be careful we don't let anyone turn us against each other."

"Agreed."

"We're in this together, right? That's what you said."

"We're in this together."

"Jack?"

"Yes?"

"Are you dangerous?"

"When I need to be."

Olive swallowed. She knew only too well there could be many kinds of danger.

Jack reached up and removed his sunglasses, folding them and then tucking them into his pocket. All the while, his gaze never left hers. His eyes were as deep and dark as the lake and just as mysterious, just as perilous. Olive could feel the tentacles of their attraction weaving a sensuous trail along her spine, heating her blood and prickling her nerve endings. All she had to do was reach over and put her hand on top of his and the conversation would be over. They would go back up the steps to the cabin, disappear into the shadowy cocoon of his bedroom and live out the fantasy that had been teasing her ever since he'd rescued her from the top of the bridge.

Her fingers tightened around the railing so that she wouldn't be tempted to touch him.

"It's good to be cautious." His words seemed to have a double meaning and Olive shivered. "With Mona Sutton, with Beth Driscoll, with everyone in this town."

"Beth Driscoll?" Olive stared at him in surprise. "What does she have to do with anything?"

"I saw her on bridge this morning. I went back to have a look around and she was at the guardrail staring down into the water. She seemed distracted. So much so that she didn't even notice my arrival. I get the distinct feeling she's a very unhappy woman."

Olive's tone turned derisive. "She's married to Tommy Driscoll. Of course, she's unhappy."

"Have you ever had any problems with Beth?"

The question stopped Olive cold. "How strange that you would ask me that now. A day ago I would have said no. We've always gotten on well. But Mona told me this morning that Beth was very upset by my appointment. She even threatened to resign. I knew there would be hard feelings, but I had no idea anyone wanted to quit, least of all Beth."

"Maybe that explains the tension I sensed when your name came up," Jack said.

"What did she say?" Olive demanded. "What did *you* say?"

The corners of his mouth twitched. "She said you had a crush on me back in the day."

Had everyone in town known about her feelings for Jack? "She actually said that?"

His eyes gleamed. "Not true?"

"Yes, it's true," Olive admitted with a shrug. "But it was just a silly schoolgirl infatuation. It didn't mean anything."

"I never thought it did."

"I was lonely and heartbroken when we first moved to Pine Lake. I'd just lost my dad. I didn't have friends or anyone I could talk to. And I felt so horribly guilty. I'm the one who begged him to drive home that night in the middle of a terrible storm. For a long time, I blamed myself for the accident. And even though my mother would never admit it, I think she did, too. It was a very bad time and you were nice to me."

"I'm glad."

Her voice turned ironic. "I know how pathetic that must sound considering you barely remembered me that first night at the bridge. But your kindness meant a lot to me. It gave me something to focus on instead of my misery. So, yes, I had a crush on you for a while, but it didn't mean anything."

"So you said."

Olive lifted her gaze to his. "How I felt then has nothing to do with the way I feel about you now."

Jack straightened from the rail, placing his bandaged hand on her shoulder. "How do you feel about me now?"

She stood on tiptoes, taking his face in her hands

as she drew his mouth to hers. It was a slow, lingering kiss. Languid and easy with the breeze rippling through her hair and the sun still warm on her skin. She slipped her hands to the back of his neck as his arms came around her waist. Their tongues touched and mingled as he pulled her into him.

The dock swayed beneath them and Olive drew away, shaking her head as if to clear her senses. "Jack?"

"Yes?"

"Let's go up the cabin."

His gaze deepened with awareness. "Are you sure?"

"Unless you'd rather do it here on the dock."

"The cabin will be good."

THE LATE AFTERNOON sunlight shone through the long windows in the living room, but the bedroom was cool and shadowy. They were both barefoot and shirtless, having left a trail of discarded clothing down the hallway. Jack pressed Olive against the wall, cupping her breasts through the lace of her bra as he kissed her again and again. She arched into him, wrapping her arms around his neck and running her fingers through the hair at his nape. His lips skimmed downward, tracing her jawline, tickling her lobe, finding the pulse point in her throat. Shivering, she fumbled with the button on his jeans and then the zipper and they laughed softly at her struggles.

"I can't seem to make my fingers work."

"They're working for me," he murmured and Olive's laugh grew breathless and throaty. There was no awkwardness between then, not even a momentary reluctance as they finished undressing.

He lifted her and she wrapped her legs around him, tunneling her fingers through his hair with a deep sigh. They fell back against the bed, Olive on top and they laughed some more as a feather floated up from the pillows and clung to her lashes. Jack tenderly plucked it away and then their expressions sobered as their gazes collided.

He rolled them, so smoothly Olive was barely aware of the motion until he was suddenly staring down at her, smiling and knowing. Her heart pounded, her every nerve ending tingled as he lowered his mouth to her breasts and then trailed his lips down her abdomen, lower and lower until she felt his tongue skim along her inner thigh.

He lingered there, kissing and teasing, until he felt her tremble and then he moved up and over her and she cupped his face, drawing his mouth to hers as she rolled him, not as smoothly, but just as eagerly. She slid down his body, her lips whispering over his abdomen, her hands stroking, her tongue exploring.

The sun had set by this time and the room had grown dim. Jack was little more than a silhouette as

Olive moved back up, positioning herself over him, taking him in with a gasp. She smiled down at him as she began to move, and then losing control all too soon, she fell forward, hands splayed against the headboard as Jack grasped her hips. The sensations intensified as their soft moans mingled. He pulled her to him, wrapping his arms around her, holding her close as they both began to shudder.

He didn't release her when it was over. If anything, his hold on her tightened. Olive buried her head in his shoulder, drinking in the scent of him, luxuriating in the intimate bond that still kept them joined.

"Jack?"

He stirred. "Yes?"

"Don't let go, okay?"

"Not a chance."

DARKNESS HAD FALLEN by the time Jack drove Olive home. He parked in her driveway and cut the lights, but kept the engine and air conditioner running as he took a quick survey of their surroundings. It was still early, just after ten, but the neighborhood already slumbered. Curtains were drawn, blinds were closed and there wasn't another car on the street. The town seemed deserted and haunted.

Olive, face scrubbed clean of makeup, hair still slightly mussed, sat watching him. In the glow of the streetlight, her freckles stood out starkly on her pale skin. Jack had never seen anything so sensuous. He wanted to trail his knuckles along her cheek, to trace her slightly parted lips with his thumb. He could still feel her against him, warm and pliant and quivering.

He draped his arm along the back of her seat, teasing the hair until he felt her shiver.

"Sure you don't want to change your mind?" he said. "You could stay with me at the lake tonight."

"You've no idea how tempted I am. But I've still got work to do and I think a little distance and perspective might be good for both of us."

"You're probably right." But his fingers continued to tease.

She sighed. "Which is why I'm not going to invite you in for a drink."

"That's a shame."

"But in case you couldn't tell, I had a really good time tonight." Her expression suddenly sobered. "Jack?"

"Yes?"

"Can I ask you a question?"

"Ask away."

"Why did you really leave the police department? You don't have to answer if you don't want to. Your past is none of my business and I know I shouldn't pry. It's just… I'd like to get to know you better. Is that wrong?"

His fingers stilled in her hair. "It's not wrong, but the answer may shock you."

Her eyes widened. "Now you have to tell me."

"I shot and killed my partner," he said with stark brevity.

She was silent for a moment. He could tell she was trying very hard to keep her expression neutral. "What happened?"

He dropped his hand to the seat. "I don't talk about it much. I can't even remember the last time the subject came up. I've always thought some things are best left in the past."

"That's an odd sentiment coming from you," she said.

He smiled. "It's a little inconsistent, I guess."

"A little inconsistent? Says the man who came back to his hometown to solve a fifteen-year-old murder."

"Long story short, we were working undercover and he set me up."

"He was dirty?"

"For years, as it turned out. The worst part was that I never saw it coming. He operated right under my nose and I didn't have a clue." He trailed his fingertip along the steering wheel. "His behavior was hard for me to reconcile. We weren't just partners, we were friends. We went through the academy together. He was the best man at my wedding and I'm godfather to one of his kids. But it came down to him or me and so I took the shot."

"No·wonder you don't trust anyone," Olive said. "Were you charged?"

"No. I was exonerated and cleared for active duty, but everything changed after the shooting. I didn't feel the same way about the department so I left."

"I get it," she said softly. "You must have wondered who else might betray you. So how did you end up in private security?"

"An acquaintance introduced me to a man named Ezra Blackthorn. He offered me a job at the Blackthorn Agency and I've been there ever since."

"Is he really ex-CIA? This Ezra Blackthorn?"

Jack turned in surprise. "Where did you hear that?"

"From Mona by way of Tommy Driscoll. She said the Caddo County Sheriff's Office has been looking into your background. Jack…" Olive placed her hand on his arm. "She didn't come right out and say it, but I got the impression that Tommy considers you a suspect."

"For what?"

"Jamie Butaud's murder."

"That's absurd," he said. "I never even met the woman."

"I know that, but if Tommy's looking for a scapegoat, your arrival in Pine Lake couldn't have been timelier."

"A scapegoat? You think he had something to do with Jamie's murder?"

Olive paused. "I never said that. I only meant he's under pressure to make an arrest just like Sheriff Brannigan was fifteen years ago. But that's not what you meant, is it?"

"Nathan thinks Tommy may have been romantically involved with Jamie going all the way back to her first arrest."

"But she was just a kid back then," Olive said. "She couldn't have been more than sixteen."

"Which would give him a powerful motive if she threatened to expose him."

Olive grew pensive. "Does Nathan have any proof of this relationship?"

"He claims he never saw them together, but Jamie supposedly has a tattoo on her shoulder that was once considered Tommy Driscoll's mark. According to Nathan, a lot of girls who had been with Tommy in high school had that tattoo—a heart with a lightning bolt through the center. I didn't say anything to Nathan, but Anna came back from a weekend trip with a similar tattoo on her hip."

Olive gasped. "You're saying that Anna and Tommy Driscoll—"

"It's possible. I don't know for certain."

She sat back against the seat. "This changes everything. If Tommy was involved with Anna, then he could have had a motive for her murder, too."

"So could I, for that matter."

"But you're innocent," she said without pause. "We don't know about Tommy. I've never liked him so I may be biased. Do you think he's capable of cold-blooded murder?"

"I wouldn't rule it out because he wears a badge."

"No, I guess you wouldn't."

"Look," Jack said. "This isn't your fight. You should go inside, lock your door and forget we had this conversation."

Olive dismissed the suggestion with a careless wave of her hand. "Don't worry about me. I know what I'm doing, too. Eyes wide open, remember?"

"Olive—"

She folded her arms. "We're in this together. That's what you said."

He sighed. "I don't want you to get hurt."

"I don't want you to get hurt, either… Jack?"

"Yes?"

"I don't care what Nathan said about tattoos and marks and Tommy Driscoll's conquests. Anna really loved you. I know she did."

He reached out and tucked back a strand of her hair. "That was all a long time ago. You don't need to worry about my feelings."

"I know."

"But I like that you do." He leaned across the console, brushing his lips against hers and then deepening the kiss the moment he felt her respond.

"It's getting late," she said when they finally broke apart. "I should go in."

"I'll walk you to the door."

"You don't have to. I set the security system before I left."

"I'd feel better if I have a look around before I go."

"Jack?"

"Yes?"

"You can come in for a nightcap if you want."

Chapter Twelve

Jack had only been gone a few minutes when a soft knock sounded on Olive's door. She was still up working on the reports she'd neglected earlier. Wondering if he'd forgotten something, she hurried to answer, taking a glance through the peephole before disarming the alarm and opening the door to her cousin.

"What are you doing here so late?" she asked in surprise.

"I'm sorry for dropping in like this," Nathan said. "I thought about calling but I didn't want to disturb you in case you'd already gone to bed. So I drove by, saw your lights on and decided to take a chance you were still up." He glanced past her into the foyer. "You alone? Can we talk for a minute?"

"Sure, come on in." She stood back so that he could enter. "What's this about?"

He shoved his hands in his pockets as if unsure where to start. "Is that fresh coffee I smell? At this hour?"

"I'm working and it's going to be a long night. You want some?"

"I was about to suggest something stronger, but coffee will do."

He followed her into the kitchen and she motioned him to the table as she got down another mug from the cupboard. "You want something to eat?" She poured his coffee and topped off her own, then turned back to the counter. "I've got cheese and crackers, some fruit."

"I'm fine."

She went back over to the table and sat down across from him. He took a drink of the coffee and grimaced. "Bitter."

"Is it? I hadn't noticed." Olive took a tentative taste. "I guess it is a little. But you didn't come over here to critique my coffee, did you?"

"Have you talked to Jack tonight? I was hoping I'd find him here."

"He left a little while ago. Why are you looking for him?" She sipped her coffee as she studied her cousin's demeanor. "What's going on, Nathan? You seem agitated."

"I don't mean to worry you, but I'm a little concerned about his whereabouts."

"Why?" she asked in alarm.

Nathan took off his glasses and wiped the lenses. His eyes looked bleary and unfocused until he put them back on. "Has he said anything to you about his blackout? Has he remembered anything about those missing hours?"

"Not that I know of. Nathan..."

"I'm getting to the point, I promise. He said the last thing he remembered was following Marc Waller's truck down Commerce. Then he remembered nothing else until the next day when I found him unconscious in the cabin with bumps and bruises that he couldn't explain."

"Yes, I know," Olive said impatiently. "I was there, remember?"

He lowered his voice. "I have contacts all over town. You know that, too, right? Nothing happens in Pine Lake that I don't hear about."

"Nathan, please—"

"Marc Waller was found murdered in the old Masonic Lodge on Commerce."

She gasped. "When?"

"The body was found earlier tonight, but he'd been dead for at least a day or two. Someone beat him up and then shot him in the back of the head."

Olive's heart thudded so hard she felt light-headed. "You're not suggesting Jack had anything to do with Marc's murder, are you?"

Nathan hesitated. "I don't know what to think. Especially in light of what the police found at the crime scene."

"What are you talking about?"

"Jack's fingerprints were all over that place."

IT WAS LATE by the time Jack got back to the cabin. His hair was still damp from Olive's shower as he climbed out of the car and took the porch steps two at a time. Then he paused at the top, attracted by a light reflected in one of the front windows. He thought at first the glow emanated from somewhere in the woods, but then he turned and realized the flash of red and blue came from a light bar atop the police car easing down the road.

The cruiser pulled into his driveway and parked. When the door opened and the red dome light came on, he recognized Tommy Driscoll.

Jack could hear the intermittent static of the radio as the Caddo County sheriff communicated with his dispatcher. Then he climbed out of the car, closed the door and stood with one hand on the hilt of his gun as he surveyed his surroundings.

His gaze lit on the porch and he drew his weapon. "Who's up there?"

"It's me." Jack moved out of the shadows to the edge of the porch. "What brings you out to the lake at this hour?" He nodded toward the gun. "I gather this isn't a social call."

"We've serious business to discuss, Jack. Come down the steps slowly and keep your hands where I can see them."

Déjà vu niggled as he descended the steps. "What's going on?"

"You armed, Jack?"

He felt the cold metal of his weapon at his back. "Yeah."

"Put it on the ground and kick it over here."

Jack did as he was told.

Tommy picked up the gun and tucked it into his waistband. "I need you to come down to the station and answer a few questions."

"About?"

"Marc Waller was found murdered earlier this evening. Someone worked him over good and then put a bullet in the back of his head. Could be a drug deal gone wrong, could be something else. He got crossways with the wrong guy, that's for damn sure."

Jack drew a steadying breath and reminded himself to remain calm. He wasn't seventeen anymore. He could handle Tommy Driscoll. "What's that got to do with me?"

"We found your fingerprints at the crime scene."

An image flashed behind Jack's eyes. He didn't remember meeting Marc Waller and yet he somehow knew what the man looked like. Tall and lanky with scraggly brown hair and a bad disposition. Jack's scraped knuckles tingled a warning as memories started to nudge him.

"You think I killed him?"

"I just need you to answer a few questions."

"If I refuse?"

Any hint of the old Tommy was obscured by the grim set of his mouth and the steely gleam in his eyes. "You don't want to do that, Jack. I could shoot you where you stand and no one would fault me. A lot of people in this town still think you killed Anna."

"Is that so?"

"You know it is. That's why you came back, isn't it? To clear your name? Instead, you've ended up in a real jam. You've already lied to me once. You and Olive both. If you refuse to cooperate, I'll have no choice but to drag her down to the station and I promise you things won't end well for her. What do you think the school board would do if they found out their new principal gave a false statement to the police in a murder investigation? She'll be canned within a week and I doubt another school district will touch her. That what you want, Jack? You want to take Olive Belmont down with you?"

Jack's hands flexed at his sides. He took another deep breath. "I'll cooperate."

"Glad to hear it. Now turn around and put your hands behind your back."

"Am I under arrest?"

"No, but I don't trust you not to try something stupid."

Jack turned and held out his arms, wincing when he heard the snap of the locks.

"You never should have come back here," Tommy said, a split second before pain exploded at the base of Jack's skull. He staggered forward, trying to stay on his feet, but the blow felled him. He crashed to the ground as shadows swirled all around him.

"I'M SORRY TO spring this on you, but I have to find Jack," Nathan said as he finished his coffee. "I wouldn't be surprised if Tommy Driscoll is already tracking him down and I need to make sure things don't get out of hand."

"Out of hand?" Olive felt sick and dazed and she couldn't seem to focus. "Jack was here earlier…"

"So you said."

"I don't—" She tried to rise and then dropped back down to her seat as a wave of dizziness washed over her.

Nathan rose and knelt in front of her. "What's wrong? You don't look so good."

"I feel light-headed. The room is spinning…" She put a hand on the table to steady her balance and knocked over her cup. She stared at the spilled coffee and then slowly brought her gaze back to Nathan. "What did you…"

"I'm sorry it had to come to this, Olive. Truly I am. You're the only person in this town I ever cared about. I tried to protect you, but once you found Anna's necklace you became another loose end."

"How did…?"

"I saw you last night. I saw you every other night that you went to the bridge, too. I've been watching you, Olive. Following you for weeks. I couldn't put my finger on it exactly, but little things you said… the way you looked at me at times… I had a bad feeling you were starting to remember."

Olive tried to swallow past the bile in her throat,

tried to form a coherent thought. She could barely focus, could barely utter a sound. But inside she was screaming. *Someone* was screaming...

ON SOME LEVEL, Olive knew she was dreaming. The screams weren't real and yet she found herself reluctantly moving toward the sound, controlled by that strange mix of urgency and inertia that only a nightmare could produce. The bridge loomed over her. She could see the truss silhouetted against the night sky, a monstrous manifestation of all her deepest fears and her darkest guilt. She didn't want to go there. She didn't want to follow those screams. Something bad was happening on that bridge. Something she didn't want to see.

Wake up, Olive! Wake up now!

But the lethargy of sleep lured her back under even as those screams pulled her toward consciousness. She floated in and out of her dream, watching figures, hearing voices...

Let her go! We can't do this, Nathan!

What do you think will happen if I let her go? She'll go straight to the cops, you idiot. Your football career will be over and no decent school will let me in. Our lives will be ruined. Don't you get that?

You said it was just a prank. A way to teach her a lesson. That's what you said. If we scared her enough, she'd leave us alone. That's what you said!

She knows all about you and that Sutton bitch.

She talks and your girlfriend goes straight to prison. That'll be on you, Tommy. Is that what you want?

Don't pretend this is about me. You're the one who planned this whole thing. You're the one who'd be in big trouble if the school ever found out you hacked into their system and changed your grades. Your old man is just looking for an excuse to disown you. Everyone in this town knows you'd be nothing but a loser without his name and money.

And you're nothing but a sniveling coward. You don't have the brains or the balls to do anything on your own. I'm the one who has to think of everything. Where do you think you're going?

Home. I've had enough of this—

Get back here! You're not going anywhere. You think you can just walk away from this? We're in this together whether you like it or not. You're the one who called Anna, remember? You're the one who convinced her that Beth was in trouble. You lured her out of her house and into your car under false pretenses. That's kidnapping, Tommy. And now you're an accomplice to murder.

She's not dead yet.

Then shut your stupid mouth and help me end this. She's coming around.

I'm not committing murder. Not for you, not for anyone.

I swear to God, if I have to—

What? What will you do? Kill me, too? This isn't

*even about Anna, is it? You did all this just so you
could get back at Jack King...*

The voices faded, replaced by an echo within Olive's dream. *Please help me, please help me, please
help me.*

A part of her wanted to wake up from the nightmare even as she felt compelled to sink deeper into
oblivion. Where she floated now was dark and silent, but she knew she wasn't alone. She could still
see those distant silhouettes. Every now and then
she heard a grunt of exertion. And then the voices
came back, one hushed with fear, the other quivering with excitement.

Is she...?

*Yeah. You should have seen the way her eyes
bulged—*

Stop it! I'm gonna be sick.

*I'd hold it if I were you. You don't want your DNA
spewed all over this bridge.*

*I need to get out of here, Nathan. Please. It's done.
Can't we just go home now?*

Help me get her clothes off first.

What?

*Relax, I'm not a perv. We need to make it look like
a sexual assault. She was with Jack earlier. They
did it in his car.*

How do you know that?

*Because I saw them, dummy. If we get lucky,
maybe there'll be some of his DNA left when the
cops find the body.*

Jesus, Nathan.

What? The boyfriend is always the number one suspect. Especially if they find her broken necklace in his vehicle. It'll look like they struggled.

You hate him that much?

Let's just say, wiping that smug look off his face will be almost as much fun as—

Stop talking. Please. Let's just get this over with.

THE MEMORY FLEETED as Nathan knelt in front of Olive to check the dilation of her pupils. She wanted to shove him away, but she couldn't lift her hands from the chair seat. "Almost there," he murmured.

He rose and grabbed some paper towels from the counter to clean up the spilled coffee. Olive tried to scream, but her tongue felt thick and heavy and she couldn't open her lips. She clutched the edge of her chair as the room spun faster and faster. Her mind clouded, but she used every ounce of her strength to keep the shadows at bay. The moment she succumbed, it would be over. The way it had been for poor Anna.

THE VOICES HAD gone silent again as Olive stepped onto the bridge. She could feel the night wind on her face, could hear the distant hoot of an owl. Consciousness was within arm's reach, but something— someone—kept pulling her back under.

Hang on, Olive. Just a little while longer. Sleep is your friend right now.

Daddy?

Shush. Sleep...

One of the silhouettes came toward her. Something dangled from his fingers. A necklace or a charm. The sparkle of the gold mesmerized her, but when he spotted her in the shadows, the chain slipped from his fingers and disappeared through a crack in the floorboards. He barely seemed to notice. He came to her slowly, calling her name.

That you, Olive? What are you doing out here? Answer me!

Shush. Sleep...

He waved a hand in front of her face. Olive? You awake? Olive!

Sleep...sleep...

OLIVE FOUGHT OFF the shadows even as lethargy lulled her. She wanted nothing so much as to close her eyes and let the darkness take her, but she could hear a voice in her head—Jack's voice now—urging her to fight. *Don't let go, Olive. Don't ever let go.*

Nathan stood over her with mounting impatience.

"Give it up, Olive. Just close your eyes and go to sleep."

She blinked rapidly to let him know she was still cognizant and defiant.

He sighed. "I should have ended it when I saw you on the bridge that night. I should never have taken a chance that you would one day remember, but I was still on such a high after Anna. I felt invincible. Like nothing could touch me. And I liked you, Olive. I liked having you around. The old man was almost decent to me with you in the house. So I took you back home, put you to bed and in all this time, your memories have stayed buried. Maybe they would never have surfaced if I'd left you well enough alone.

"But I got restless. Father was content to be a big fish in a small pond, but not me. I want more. You can understand that, can't you? I don't want to forever be known as *his* son. I want to make my own mark. Achieve what he never had the guts to do. But Tommy was always going to be a problem. So long as we were both in Pine Lake, I could keep him in line, but the higher I climbed, the lower he sank. He would always be there with his threats and bribes, needing me to clean up his messes. So I started making plans, figuring out the best way to eliminate the problem without incriminating myself. And one day, the solution fell right into my lap."

Nathan finished mopping up the coffee and threw away the paper towels.

"I had lunch with Jack's old attorney about another case. Jack's name came up. Imagine my surprise when he told me that they still kept in touch and that neither of them had ever believed Wayne Foukes was guilty. He said Jack would never rest until the truth came out. Right then and there, I decided that Jack King would have to come back to Pine Lake and kill Tommy Driscoll."

JACK FOUGHT HIS way up out of the darkness. He could
hear voices nearby, but the pounding in his head
muted the sound. He knew at once where he was. The
floorboards swayed beneath him as the truss creaked
and rattled above him. His right wrist had been handcuffed to the guardrail of the old Pine Lake Bridge.

A few feet away, someone lay motionless near the
edge. It took Jack a moment to put it together—the
slight body, the copper-colored hair.

"Olive!" He whispered her name. "Olive, can you
hear me?"

She didn't answer.

"Olive!"

He yanked at the cuffs and then forced himself to
remain still as he concentrated on the voices.

"I did as you wanted," Tommy Driscoll said an-
grily. "I got him out here, didn't I? The rest is up to
you. I don't want any part of it."

"Tommy, Tommy." Nathan's voice was decep-
tively soft, dangerously persuasive. "How many
times do I have to remind you that we're in this together? Just like old times. It's in both our best interests that Jack not be allowed to leave Pine Lake
alive."

"Jack is one thing. What about Olive?"

"She's become too much of a liability, I'm afraid."

"For God's sake, Nathan, you can't keep killing
people. First Jamie and then Marc Waller. And now
this. Even I can't whitewash four bodies."

"You can do anything you want. That's why I

helped get you elected. Despite our clashes and your backstabbing, we've both benefitted from our arrangement. We've each turned a blind eye when we needed to. All that would have ended if Jamie had made your affair public. You should be thanking me for cleaning up another of your messes."

"Thanking you? For murdering someone I cared about?"

"You'll get over it. And as for Marc Waller, what were you thinking, paying him to terrorize Olive? You thought you could manipulate me by threatening my cousin, but when has that ever worked out for you, Tommy? All you accomplished was to open yourself up to blackmail. And once again I had to clean up after you. Marc Waller's blood is on your hands, too, so get off your high horse and let's end this once and for all."

"What do you want me to do?"

"You brought Jack's gun?"

A moment of silence while Jack imagined his weapon changing hands.

"I still say you should have left well enough alone," Tommy said sullenly. "Everything was fine until you brought him back here."

"Everything was *not* fine. He was never going to rest until he solved Anna's murder."

"You say that, but he hadn't been back in fifteen years."

"He would have come back eventually. Wouldn't

you, Jack?" Nathan turned to peer at Jack through the darkness. "It was always going to come to this."

Jack didn't answer.

"Look at it this way." He came over and hunkered on the bridge just out of Jack's reach. "Now you get to go out the hero."

Jack slowly lifted his head. "There's only one way that can happen."

Nathan grinned. "You've figured it out, haven't you?"

"It's your plan so not exactly rocket science."

The smile vanished as Nathan stood, aiming the gun at Jack's head. "You're the one who's going to expose Anna's killer after all these years. Like I said, you'll get to be the hero. Unfortunately, a dead hero, but your name will finally be cleared. That must give you some satisfaction."

"What the hell are you talking about?" Tommy stalked into Jack's periphery.

"You need to have a little talk with your partner. Nathan's gone to a lot of trouble to set you up, Tommy."

"Set *me* up? You're the one handcuffed to the bridge."

"No, he's right." Nathan turned. "You're just too dumb to figure it out. First you killed Anna and now you've gone and killed Jamie Butaud and Marc Waller."

Tommy tried to draw his weapon, but Nathan was

quicker. He spun and fired two rounds straight at Tommy's heart. He dropped with barely a sound.

Jack shifted so that he could keep Olive in his line of sight. She didn't make a sound, hadn't moved a muscle. Either she was out cold or—

Nathan said with chilling aplomb, "You'll notice that I shot him with your gun, Jack. You found out he killed Anna and confronted him. He drew his weapon and it was either him or you. Just like with your old partner. Photographs of Jamie will be found in his possession, along with Anna's necklace. Thank you for finding that, by the way."

"You haven't missed a trick, have you?"

"I've always been a lot smarter than you, Jack. This just proves it. You want to know the real beauty of my plan? Nothing will touch me. I checked into a Dallas hotel this morning. I had lunch with old friends and pre-dinner drinks with a colleague before attending a fundraiser. Now I'm fast asleep in my room where the police will likely awaken me in the morning to tell me about poor Olive."

He moved away from Jack. His focus now was on retrieving Tommy's weapon. He turned his back on Olive and her hand shot out to snake around his ankle. He lost his balance and crashed to the floor but not before he'd kicked Olive aside. She rolled beneath the guardrail, clutching the floorboards with a gasp.

Jack's left hand shot out helplessly. "Hang on.

Hang on. Hang on," he said under his breath as Olive clung to the edge of the bridge.

Nathan was picking himself up, reaching for the gun...

As Jack tore at his restraint, a movement to his right caught his eye. Something glinted in Tommy Driscoll's outstretched hand...the handcuff key...

Jack strained toward the key even as his wrist screamed in protest. He had the key between his fingers. *Don't drop it, don't drop it, don't drop it...*

He was free, lunging for Olive with one hand as he grabbed Tommy's weapon with the other. "I've got you," he said as he turned and fired.

Chapter Thirteen

The next two days passed in a blur of police interrogations. Olive barely saw Jack. When the dust finally settled, she drove out to the cabin late one afternoon and they had drinks on the dock as they watched the sunset.

The last thing she wanted to do was rehash what had happened. What more could be said? Nathan and Tommy had killed Anna and then given each other an alibi. The secret had eventually destroyed their friendship even as it had kept them dependent on one another until Nathan had decided to break free.

A breeze picked up as twilight moved in from the pinewoods. Out on the lake, a loon trilled a warning. Olive shivered as she searched Jack's profile.

"I was allowed to see Nathan today," she told him.

He turned. "How did that go?"

"As you might expect. He shows no remorse. Quite the opposite, in fact. He seems rather proud of the way he's manipulated people in this town for years, especially those closest to him. Tommy, Mona,

Beth Driscoll. Me most of all, I think. I can't believe I never saw the real Nathan. I trusted him. I always thought he had my back."

"He fooled a lot of people," Jack said. "He knew as soon as he made that call to me, I'd come back here to search for Anna's killer. He played me, too, Olive."

"He did say one thing that I think you should know. Jack…" She put her hand on his arm. "Anna never cheated on you with Tommy. Nathan saw her tattoo that night on the bridge when he tore off her clothes. He made up the story about Tommy's 'mark' so that you would go after him even harder."

"What about Jamie Butaud's tattoo? He didn't make that up. I saw the autopsy report."

"No, but he manipulated her into getting a similar tattoo. Even then, he was laying the groundwork to frame Tommy. The heart tattoos connected the victims. Or maybe Nathan just got a sick thrill out of seeing Anna's tattoo on Jamie Butaud. I don't know. But Tommy wasn't innocent. He could have stopped Anna's murder. He could have been faithful to Beth instead of having an affair with Mona Sutton and then later going after a troubled young woman like Jamie. He made it too easy for Nathan. I guess we all did." Olive paused, tucking a strand of hair behind her ear. "I just wanted you to know about Anna."

Jack touched his knuckles to her cheek.

"Jack?"

"Yes?"

"Nathan said that Tommy hired Marc Waller to come after me."

"He thought he could somehow control Nathan by threatening you."

"That explains the incident in front of the coffee shop, but who was in the dark sedan that almost ran me down before you got to town?"

"Could have been Waller, then, too, or Beth Driscoll. She drives a dark sedan and she had an ax to grind. She'll deny it, of course, but I wouldn't be surprised if she's always known the truth about Anna. Or at least suspected."

"Mona must have suspected, too. I have to wonder if it was Tommy in her office the other day trying to coerce her into remaining silent."

"Maybe it was the other way around," Jack said.

"Another maybe," Olive said with a faint smile. "Will we ever know the whole truth?"

"One can hope. Nathan's trial should prove interesting."

"What happens in the meantime?"

"He'll be incarcerated once he's released from the hospital. After everything he's done, he won't get bail."

"That's not what I meant." Olive paused. "I mean what happens to us? You and me. School will be starting soon and you'll be heading back to Houston. After everything we've been through, do we just say goodbye?"

His gaze deepened. "What do you want to happen, Olive?"

"I don't know," she answered truthfully. "I know I don't want you to leave town."

"Even if I plan to come back?"

"For the trial, you mean."

"Before that." Jack stared out over the water for a moment. "I've decided to hang on to the cabin. I'll need a place to stay when the trial starts, and in the meantime, I can drive up on weekends and holidays. Maybe you can come down to Houston now and then."

"Are you suggesting a long-distance relationship?"

"For now. Until we can sort things out. I care about you, Olive. I may even be falling in love with you." He brought her hand to his lips. "I don't want to lose you."

"I don't want to lose you, either." She entwined her fingers with his and squeezed his hand.

"Olive?"

"Yes?"

"Don't let go, okay?"

She smiled. "Not a chance."

* * * * *

INTRIGUE

Available October 17, 2017

#1743 SHADOWS IN THE NIGHT
The Finnegan Connection • by Heather Graham
FBI special agent Micah Fox isn't accustomed to working with civilians, but criminologist Harley Frasier may be the next target after her mentor is murdered in this pulse-pounding new thriller from *New York Times* bestselling author Heather Graham.

#1744 COLTON K-9 COP
The Coltons of Shadow Creek • by Addison Fox
It isn't easy for quiet accountant Bellamy Reeves to open herself to trust, but she might have to make an exception for K-9 bomb squad officer Donovan Colton and his adorable dog when her life threatens to explode—literally.

#1745 DADDY DEFENDER
Omega Sector: Under Siege • by Janie Crouch
Someone has placed widow Summer Worrall and her small daughter in their crosshairs...but lucky for Summer, Ashton Fitzgerald isn't the handsome and unassuming handyman she thought he was. He's a highly trained sharpshooter intent on keeping his found family safe.

#1746 RELUCTANT HERO
by Debra Webb & Regan Black
It's bad enough for a security expert to be threatened over gold stolen during his unit's last mission in Iraq—a theft of which he's innocent. But to make matters worse, reporter Rebecca Wallace comes in harm's way while investigating him. Can he keep her safe and maintain his innocence in the line of fire?

#1747 MR. TAKEN
Mystery Christmas • by Danica Winters
Firefighter Colter Fitzgerald knows that Whitney Barstow has been burned in the past, but when Dunrovin ranch is targeted by an arsonist, can she face the fires of his passion? Or will their future go up in smoke?

#1748 SMALL-TOWN FACE-OFF
The Protectors of Riker County • by Tyler Anne Snell
Mara Copeland was born and raised in a world of criminals, so how could she face a future with Sheriff Billy Reed? But when she returns to Riker County with a child in her arms and trouble in hot pursuit, it's time to see where allegiances really lie...

Get 2 Free Books,
Plus 2 Free Gifts—
just for trying the Reader Service!

⊕ HARLEQUIN
I N T R I G U E

Vickie reached out and set her hand over Monica's. "I'm so sorry."

Monica Verne looked at Vickie and nodded. Griffin thought that Vickie's ability to feel with others and offer them real comfort was going to be one of her greatest assets in joining the Krewe. It was also going to be one of the most difficult parts of the job for her to learn to manage. He lowered his head for a moment; it was an odd time to smile. And an odd time to think just how lucky he was. Vickie was beautiful to look at—five foot eight, with long raven black waves of hair and blue-green eyes that could change and shimmer like emeralds.

She was also so caring—honest and filled with integrity.

He truly loved her. Watching her empathy and gentle touch with Monica, he knew all the more reason why.

"My husband didn't kill himself!" Monica whispered fervently.

"I don't think it's been suggested that he killed himself.

I believe they're considering it an accidental death," Griffin began.

"Accidental death, my ass! If there's any last thing I can do for Franklin, it's going to be to make someone prove that this was no accidental death!" Monica lashed out, indignant. She wasn't angry with Vickie—who was still holding her hand. Her passion was against the very suggestion that her husband's death had been through a simple slip—some misfortune.

She wagged a finger at Griffin. "You listen to me, and listen well. We were the best, Frankie and me. I swear it. When all else fell to hell and ruin, we still had one another… Franklin did not meet up with a friend! He did not break into that cellar to drink himself to death! I'm telling you, I knew my husband, he…"

She broke off, gritting her teeth. She was trying not to cry. The woman was truly in anguish; she was also furious.

"I don't know when he went out. I don't know why he went out—or how he wound up at the restaurant. I do know one thing."

"What is that, Mrs. Verne?" Vickie asked.

Monica Verne startled them both, slamming a fist on the coffee table. "My husband was murdered!"

The motion seemed to be a cue.

In the yard, a dozen birds took flight, shrieking and cawing.

Griffin could see them as they let out their cries, sweeping into the sky.

A murder of crows…

And an unkindness of ravens…

As poetically cruel as the death of Franklin Verne.

WICKED DEEDS
by New York Times *bestselling author Heather Graham.*
Available now from MIRA® Books.

www.Harlequin.com

NEW YORK TIMES BESTSELLING AUTHOR

HEATHER GRAHAM

WICKED

KREWE OF HUNTERS

DEEDS

Romance and suspense in perfect combination!
—*Library Journal on Flawless*

$8.99 U.S./$10.99 CAN.

$1.⁰⁰ OFF

New York Times bestselling author

HEATHER GRAHAM

returns with the next
action-packed romantic suspense story
in the *Krewe of Hunters* series.

WICKED DEEDS

Available now.

mira

Harlequin.com

---✂

$1.⁰⁰ OFF the purchase price of WICKED DEEDS by Heather Graham.

Offer valid from September 19, 2017, to October 31, 2017.
Redeemable at participating retail outlets, in-store only. Not redeemable at
Barnes & Noble. Limit one coupon per purchase. Valid in the U.S.A. and Canada only.

52615115

5 65373 00076 2 (8100)0 12306

® and ™ are trademarks owned and used by the trademark owner and/or its licensee.

© 2017 Harlequin Enterprises Limited

MCOUPHGI017

She prayed for sleep, but her mind kept returning to that time
in the Sahara. Being part of the expedition had been such a
privilege. She remembered the way they'd all felt when they'd
broken through to the tomb. Satima Mahmoud—the pretty
Egyptian interpreter who had so enchanted Joe Rosello—had
been the first to scream when the workers found the entry.

Of course, Henry Tomlinson was called then. He'd been
there to break the seal. They'd all laughed and joked about
the curses that came with such finds, about the stupid movies
that had been made.

Yes, people had died during other expeditions—as if they
had been cursed. The Tut story was one example—and yet,
by all accounts, there had been scientific explanations for
everything that'd happened.

Almost everything, anyway.

And their find…

There hadn't been any curses. Not written curses, at any
rate.

But Henry had died. And Henry had broken the seal…

No mummy curse had gotten to them; someone had killed
Henry. And that someone had gotten away with it because

neither the American Department of State nor the Egyptian government had wanted the expedition caught in the crosshairs of an insurgency. Reasonably enough!

But now…

For some reason, the uneasy dreams that came with her restless sleep weren't filled with mummies, tombs, sarcophagi or canopic jars. No funerary objects whatsoever, no golden scepters, no jewelry, no treasures.

Instead, she saw the sand. The endless sand of the Sahara. And the sand was teeming, rising up from the ground, swirling in the air.

Someone was coming…

She braced, because there were rumors swirling along with the sand. Their group could fall under attack—there was unrest in the area. Good Lord, they were in the Middle East!

But she found herself walking through the sand, toward whomever or whatever was coming.

She saw someone.

The killer?

She kept walking toward him. There was more upheaval behind the man, sand billowing dark and heavy like a twister of deadly granules.

Then she saw him.

And it was Micah Fox.

She woke with a start.

And she wondered if he was going to be her salvation…

Or a greater danger to her heart, a danger she hadn't yet seen.

Don't miss
SHADOWS IN THE NIGHT,
available November 2017 wherever
Harlequin® Intrigue books and ebooks are sold.

www.Harlequin.com